## Sometimes merely waiting to speak, holding back, made every word I said seem like a gem.

I was ordered to see the school psychologist when I was in ninth grade. Mama and Daddy had to come too, and Mama was asked to come back. She didn't want to, but the principal made her do it. Mostly the psychologist asked questions and I either ignored him or gave him as simple an answer as I could.

I was smart enough to realize that the psychologist had a theory that I was trying to remain invisible because my mother didn't want to be a mother and my existence reminded her she was. I had to admit to myself I had stood by quietly many times when I was much younger and wished I was invisible, especially when Mama told new friends I wasn't really her child. She'd lie and say I was her younger sister's child, a sister who was promiscuous, and she was just keeping me for a few years....

### *ICE*

## V.C. Andrews® Books

**The Dollanganger Family Series**
Flowers in the Attic
Petals on the Wind
If There Be Thorns
Seeds of Yesterday
Garden of Shadows

**The Casteel Family Series**
Heaven
Dark Angel
Fallen Hearts
Gates of Paradise
Web of Dreams

**The Cutler Family Series**
Dawn
Secrets of the Morning
Twilight's Child
Midnight Whispers
Darkest Hour

**The Landry Family Series**
Ruby
Pearl in the Mist
All That Glitters
Hidden Jewel
Tarnished Gold

My Sweet Audrina
(does not belong to a series)

**The Logan Family Series**
Melody
Heart Song
Unfinished Symphony
Music in the Night
Olivia

**The Orphans Miniseries**
Butterfly
Crystal
Brooke
Raven
Runaways (full-length novel)

**The Wildflowers Miniseries**
Misty
Star
Jade
Cat
Into the Garden (full-length novel)

**The Hudson Family Series**
Rain
Lightning Strikes
Eye of the Storm
The End of the Rainbow

**The Shooting Stars Series**
Cinnamon
Ice

Published by POCKET BOOKS

POCKET BOOKS

New York   London   Toronto   Sydney   Singapore

Following the death of Virginia Andrews, the Andrews family worked with a carefully selected writer to organize and complete Virginia Andrews' stories and to create additional novels, of which this is one, inspired by her storytelling genius.

An *Original* Publication of POCKET BOOKS

POCKET BOOKS, a division of Simon & Schuster, Inc.
1230 Avenue of the Americas, New York, NY 10020

Copyright © 2001 by the Vanda General Partnership

ISBN: 0-671-03994-6

First Pocket Books paperback printing August 2001

10  9  8  7  6  5  4  3  2  1

V.C. ANDREWS and VIRGINIA ANDREWS are registered trademarks of the Vanda General Partnership.

POCKET and colophon are registered trademarks of Simon & Schuster, Inc.

Front cover illustration by Lisa Falkenstern

Printed in the U.S.A.

# Prologue

—m—

When I was a little more than six years old, my first-grade teacher, Mrs. Waite, pulled me aside after school to tell me that if I didn't talk, if I didn't answer questions in class, and if I continued to behave like a mute, all the thoughts in my head that should have been spoken would eventually expand, explode and split my head apart.

"Just like an egg!"

"There's a warehouse in your brain for storing thoughts, but there's just so much room in there," she explained. "You've got to let more thoughts out and the only way to do that is to speak. Do you understand me, Ice?" she asked.

Mrs. Waite always grimaced when she pronounced my name and spoke through clenched teeth as if she hated it and as if simply pronouncing it made her teeth chatter with the chill.

During the one and only parent-teacher conference Mama attended when I was in grade school, Mrs. Waite questioned the wisdom of naming me Ice. I was sitting there in my little desk and chair with my hands clasped (as they were supposed to be every morning when our day began) listening to her talk about me as if I was listening to her talk about someone else. It embarrassed me, so I turned my attention to a sparrow pacing impatiently back and forth on the window ledge.

I really was more interested in the sparrow. I imagined it being bothered by our presence and wondering why human beings were here making human noises, interrupting her private singing rehearsal.

"It's more of a nickname than a name," Mrs. Waite said aggressively. "Doesn't she have another name, a real name?"

"That is her real name." Mama turned her lips in when she spoke. She did that whenever she was very angry. Her ebony eyes practically glowed with rage.

It was enough to intimidate my petite teacher who wasn't much bigger than some of her students. She was barely five feet tall with childlike features and very slim. She cowered back in her chair and glanced at me and then at Mama who kept her eyes fixed on her as if deciding whether or not she would lean forward and slap her on the side of the head.

"What do you mean by asking me if my daughter has a real name?"

"Well, I...just...wondered," she stuttered, instantly backpedaling, "I mean, she gets teased a great deal by the other students. I thought if we could do something about it now, she would avoid any of that as she grows up. You know how cruel other children can be, Mrs. Goodman."

"She'll take care of herself just fine," Mama replied, twisted her lips, nodded at me and then stood up. "Is that it?"

"Oh no," Mrs. Waite cried, "no. Please don't leave just yet," she pleaded.

Mama took a deep breath, lifting her very feminine shoulders and firm breasts. She was proud of her beautiful figure and wouldn't wear a bra even to a school conference. Mama had me when she was only eighteen, and despite her smoking and drinking, she could still pass for a high-school senior. Her complexion was as smooth as the color of a fresh coffee bean. Daddy, who was a big, burly man with a stark black mustache that began to show some gray hairs before he was even thirty, was often teased about having a child bride or bringing his daughter around. Mama loved that. In fact, Daddy would occasionally accuse her of deliberately dressing and acting like a teenager just so it would happen. Mama would spin around on him and vent her outrage; the words flung at him so fast and sharply, they were like a handful of rocks.

"What are you accusing me of, Cameron Goodman? Huh? What are you saying about me? You saying I'm some sort of street girl? Huh? Well? What?"

Daddy would throw up his hands, shake his head and step back.

"You do what you want," he'd say.

"And what are you looking at me like that for?" she would ask me while I stood in the corner watching them argue. I didn't say anything. I stared at her and then went back to whatever I was doing.

Their arguments weren't pleasant to hear or to watch, but they weren't yet having the all-out, slam-bang quarrels they would have when I was older. That was to come. It loomed in the shadows and corners of our Philadelphia apartment like bats sleeping, waiting to be nudged, disturbed. Eventually, they circled us on an almost daily basis, eager to swoop in at the slightest sign of dissension.

"What else do you want me to know about my daughter? She sass you?" Mama asked Mrs. Waite.

"Oh no, Mrs. Goodman. I couldn't ask for a more polite child."

"So then?"

Mrs. Waite looked at me and leaned toward my mother as if she was going to whisper, only she didn't. She wanted me to hear it all.

4

"It's nice to have a shy girl these days. So many of the youngsters lack decorum."

"What's that?" Mama asked with narrow eyes of suspicion.

"Good behavior, respect for their elders. Too many of them are loud and undisciplined."

"Don't I know," Mama said bobbing her head. "Especially that Edith Merton. I tell Ice to keep away from her. She can only learn bad habits from a girl like that. I know she smokes. Right, Ice?"

I nodded.

"And she's only what? Nine? Huh?"

I gazed at the two of them. Mama knew how old Edith Merton was.

"What I was starting to say, Mrs. Goodman, is it's nice that Ice is a well-behaved girl, but she's too introverted."

"Intro- what?"

"She's reluctant to communicate, to express herself. It worries me and I've told her so many times, so this isn't a tale told out of school," Mrs. Waite said looking at me.

"Tale told out of school? We're in school," Mama pointed out and laughed. "Ain't that right, Ice?" She winked at me. "So what is it you want me to do, Mrs. Waite? I'm not following you here."

"If she continues to be so reluctant to talk, to express herself, we'll have to have her tested by the school psychologist," Mrs. Waite warned. "Not that it's a bad thing to have that done," she quickly added. "Because we've got to be concerned."

"Psychologist?" Mama pulled the corner of her lips in, puffing out her cheeks. "You saying something's wrong with her mind?"

"Something is keeping her all locked up inside," Mrs. Waite insisted. "The technical term for her problem is elective mutism."

"Elective?" She grimaced with confusion. "You mean like voting?"

"Precisely. She's choosing to be this way."

Mama raised her eyebrows. She kept them trimmed pencil thin, tweezing them almost daily because she believed the eyebrows were the most important facial feature. It was practically a religious ritual for her. She'd light incense on her vanity table and begin, humming or listening to her New Age music because the girl down at the beauty shop told her it took stress lines out of your face. Mama stared at her image in the glass and checked every inch of herself. Her gilded-framed oval mirror was her altar.

"She's choosing to be a mute? How do you know that?"

"Because she has no physical disability or language problems. In other words, no clear reason for being like she is."

"So why do you want her to see that psychosomething?"

"To evaluate her more and see if we can help her overcome whatever it is that keeps her so closed up." Carefully, now close to a real whisper, Mrs. Waite asked, "How is she at home?"

"She's a good girl there, too," Mama said, looking at me. "She knows she better be," she added filling her voice with threat. It was like blowing air into a balloon and then letting it out. She shook her head. "Election mute. That girl talks when she wants and she certainly doesn't keep her mouth shut when it's time to sing. She's the best singer in the children's church choir, you know? The minister told me so himself about a thousand times."

"No," Mrs. Waite said, her eyes wide with surprise. "Really?" She looked at me as if she had just realized I was there. "She sings?"

"The minister calls her Angel Voice. She takes after my side," Mama said proudly. "My mama was a church singer, too. Okay," she said standing again, only this time with more determination. Her quick movement sent the sparrow flying from the window ledge.

"Ice," Mama snapped.

I looked up at her.

"You talk more in school. You hear me? Don't make me mad now."

I continued to stare up at her.

"Look at the girl. She look afraid? No. She look upset? No. Don't you see, Mrs. Waite? She got ice in

7

her veins. She's as cool as can be. She never cries even when she gets slapped. She didn't cry much when she was a baby either. That's why her name fits her, no matter what you say about it. I gotta go," she added after looking at her watch. "C'mon," she told me and I rose to follow her, looking back at Mrs. Waite who shook her head and bit down on her lower lip, frustrated. Mine was probably her worst parent-teacher conference.

My reluctance to talk didn't affect my schoolwork. I wasn't a bad student. I did well on all the written work assigned and on all our tests. When I had to recite something, I did it reluctantly, but at least I did it, even though I did only what was required and spoke so softly it was nearly impossible to hear me. Mrs. Waite often complained that I never raised my hand to ask a question. If I had to go to the bathroom, I just got up and went for the bathroom pass.

"You should ask first," Mrs. Waite said. She wanted to hear me speak so much, she tried forbidding me to take the pass without asking and she soon saw that I would endure the pain of holding it in more than the pain of speaking. When she saw the agony in my eyes and saw how I squirmed in my chair, she finally offered the pass and I hurried out to do my thing.

Mrs. Waite was clairvoyant when it came to her predictions about my future in school, however. It never took my classmates long to begin teasing me after the start of a new school year. My reluctance to speak, to read aloud, to recite anything drew quick, curious and critical eyes. My behavior, along with my name, gave my tormentors a warehouse full of tortures to afflict.

I don't know how many times I heard someone in one of my classes say, "Her name's Ice because all the words are frozen in her mouth."

Once, when I was in the seventh grade, a group of girls decided they would make me talk for as long as a minute. They ganged up on me in the girls' locker room after our teacher went to see about a sick student. They stripped off my gym uniform and held me down dangling my clothes around me and threatening to keep me naked until I spoke for the full minute. Thelma Williams held up her wrist and called off the numbers on her watch.

"Talk," they chanted, "talk."

"Or we'll throw all your clothes and your uniform out the window and push you into the hallway."

"Talk!"

I cried and struggled, but they were relentless. Finally, I closed my eyes and began to sing an old Negro spiritual:

> *"I'm gonna sing when the spirit says, 'Sing!'*
> *I'm gonna sing when the spirit says, 'Sing!'*
> *I'm gonna sing when the spirit says, 'Sing,'*
> *And obey the spirit of the Lord!*

*I'm gonna pray, I'm gonna pray all night,*
*All day, angels watching me, my Lord.*
*All night, all day, and obey the spirit of the*
*Lord!*
*I'm gonna shout, shout, shout*
*When the spirit says, 'shout, shout, shout.' "*

"Shut her up!" Thelma Williams cried. She was in the church choir, too, and couldn't stand that I was singing one of our hymns. It actually frightened her and some of the others, who quickly released my arms and legs and dropped my things at my feet.

"She's nuts. Leave her be," Carla Thompson declared. It satisfied most of them and they left me alone for a while.

As I grew older, I became a little less introverted, but I was never as talkative as the other girls in my classes. Once, when another one of my teachers remarked about my quiet way, a boy named Balwin Noble—who played piano so well he was the pianist for our school chorus—said, "She's just saving her vocal cords for when it counts the most."

I looked at him and thought, maybe I was.

Maybe that was something I did naturally.

It just seemed to me that words flew all around me as undistinguished as flies with just a few as graceful and important as birds. I didn't talk just to hear the sound of my own voice or need to talk in order to make myself seem important. Silence was often a two-edged sword. It worked well by keeping me invisible, almost forgotten when and where I wanted to be forgotten. Sometimes merely waiting to speak, holding back, made every word I said seem like a gem. People listened to me more because I spoke less, whether they were my teachers or my friends.

Finally, the second of Mrs. Waite's predictions came true. I was ordered to see the school psychologist when I was in the ninth grade. Mama and Daddy had to come too, and Mama was asked to come back. She didn't want to, but the principal made her do it. I met with the psychologist a half dozen times afterward. Mostly he asked questions and I either ignored him or gave him as simple an answer as I could.

I was smart enough to realize that the psychologist, Doctor Lisa, had a theory that I was trying hard to remain invisible because my mother didn't want to be a mother and my existence reminded her she was. I had to admit to myself I had stood by quietly many times when I was much younger and wished I was invisible, especially when Mama told new friends I wasn't really her child. She'd lie and say I was her younger sister's child, a sister who was promiscuous, and she was just keeping me for a few years. She hated taking me places with her, and Daddy was often left home watching me while Mama went shopping or out to the movies with some girlfriends.

I could count on my fingers how many times we did anything as a family, especially when I was very little. Whenever Daddy offered to take us out to eat, Mama would complain, "What kind of night out is it with a child, sitting at a table with a high chair in a restaurant and either you or me having to feed her? We'll get a baby-sitter."

Mama was never terribly particular about the baby-sitter either. Any warm body old enough to carry me out in case of fire or use a telephone was considered good enough. I was often left shut up in my room, ignored or put to bed hours before I was supposed to be asleep. Many of the baby-sitters had girlfriends or boyfriends over. When I was only seven, I saw Nona Lester letting her boyfriend fondle her breasts and put his hand up her skirt. They seemed to think it was funny to have me as an audience.

Did all this cause me to be an elective mute?

I never talked about any of it. I kept it to myself, swallowed it down like some bad-tasting medicine and tried to keep it from ever coming back up. Some of it did, of course. Some of it rode in the nightmare train that rattled and rushed through my dreams making me toss and turn and wake in a sweat with a small cry.

Sometimes the cry brought Daddy, if he wasn't working at night. It never brought Mama.

No wonder I thought I hadn't even uttered a sound.

What difference did any sound make?

Silence greeted me; I greeted it back with silence. It was like staring someone down.

The darkness backed off. The train of nightmares came to a halt. I lowered my head to the pillow, took a deep breath and closed my eyes again.

Music entered, seeped into my mind from every available opening until my head was an auditorium in which a full orchestra played and I began to sing.

My voice transcended every ugly sound. I couldn't hear car horns, people screaming at each other or screaming in fear. I was traveling high above it all, floating on the notes.

Music gave words their souls.

What was the point in using them without it?

I used to wish real life was an opera or a musical like *The Phantom of the Opera* in which everyone sang when he or she spoke.

Mama would be the elective mute then.

Most unhappy and mean people would. They actually hated the sound of their own voices.

Not me.

I just kept it special, kept it waiting in the wings, waiting for the music.

# 1

—m—

# Mama's Plan

**W**henever I was alone in our apartment, which was quite often, and if I was very quiet, I could hear the sounds of other families below and around us. They traveled through the thin walls and in or over the pipes. I could move my ear from the wall on one side of the room to the other or take myself to another room, preferably the bathroom or kitchen, and press my ear to the walls there and hear different noises—what I thought of as the symphony of the Garden Apartments. It was almost like changing stations on a radio.

There were families who always seemed to be at war with each other, complaining, screaming, threatening in growls and shouts. There were those who spoke softly, enjoyed some laughter and even some singing. And there were often the sounds of someone crying, even sobbing, as if someone was walled in forever like in the short story by Edgar Allan Poe. Of course, I could hear television sets and hip-hop music. There were at least a half-dozen white families in our project, but their music wasn't very different, and I often heard as much shouting and crying from them as well.

I didn't know any other person who paid as much attention to the symphony of the Garden Apartments as I did. They were too busy making their own noises to listen to anyone else's and rarely did an hour pass in their homes when silence wasn't broken. Silence, I learned early on, frightens people, or at least makes them feel very uncomfortable. The worst punishment imposed on my school friends seemed to be keeping them in detention, forcing them to be still and shutting them off from any communication. They squirmed, grimaced, put their heads down and waited as if spiders had been released inside them and were crawling up and down their stomachs and under their chests. When the bell that dismissed them finally rang, they would burst out like an explosion of confetti in every direction, each talking louder than the other, some even screaming so hard that veins strained and popped against the skin in their temples.

Mama wasn't any different. The moment she entered the apartment, she turned on the radio or clicked on the television set, crying, "Why is this place like a morgue?"

If she had done some drinking with a girlfriend, she would dance and laugh, calling to me to join her while she fixed dinner; if I didn't come or if I made a reluctant face, she would pounce on me and accuse me of being strange, which she blamed on my daddy and his side of the family.

"Never seen a name fit better than the name I gave you, girl," she would declare. "The only time I ever see a smile on your face is when you're singing in that church. You going to be a nun or something? Wake up. Shake your booty. You got a nice figure, honey. You're lucky you don't take after your daddy in looks and be big boned like that Tania Gotchuck or somebody similar.

"You got my nose and mouth and you're getting my figure," she said with her hands on her hips, turning as if she were surrounded by mirrors.

Mama didn't need mirrors to look at herself though. She could spot her reflection in a glass on the table or a piece of silverware and suddenly fix her hair or touch her face and complain about aging too quickly. She wasn't. She was just anticipating it with such dread that the illusion of some tiny wrinkle forming or a single gray hair put hysteria into her eyes and panic in her voice.

"You wouldn't be so crazy nervous about yourself if we had another child," Daddy told her. "It would give you something more important to worry about."

He might as well have lit a firecracker in the mid-

dle of our living room, but for as long as I could remember, Daddy wanted to have more children. I
know he wanted a son badly. However, Mama grum-
bled that giving birth to me had added a half-inch or
so to her hips and another child would surely turn her
into another one of those "walruses waddling around
here with a trail of drippy-nosed brats they couldn't
afford to have. Not me. I'm still young enough to turn
a head or two."

"That's all that makes you happy, Lena," Daddy
retorted. "Being the center of attention."

He didn't make it sound like any sort of accusation or even a criticism. It was just a matter-of-fact
statement. Even so, Mama would go off on one of her
tirades about how he wanted her to be fat and ugly so
other men wouldn't look longingly at her anymore.

"You used to be proud to have me hanging on your
arm, Cameron Goodman. I could see how you would
strut like a rooster, parading me in front of your
friends, bragging with your eyes. I let you wear me
like some piece of jewelry and I didn't bitch about it,
did I? So why are you complaining now?"

"I'm not complaining, Lena, but there's more to
life now. We're settled down. We have a home, a
child. We should be building on this family, too,"
Daddy pleaded, his big hands out, palms up like
someone begging for a handout of affection and love.

"I told you a hundred times if I told you once,
Cameron. We can't have any more children on your

salary," she replied and turned away quickly to end the argument or to run from it.

That wasn't fair or even a good excuse. Daddy made a decent salary. He had always done well. Now he was the head of security for Cobbler's Market, a big department store on Ninth Street. He had been a military policeman in the army; after he came out, he started working different security positions until he was chosen to head up one and then another.

It wasn't just his size that recommended him for the job, even though he stood six feet four and weighed two hundred and twenty-five pounds. He was considered a clear-thinking, sensible man who could manage other men. I know for sure that his calm, patient demeanor helped him get along with Mama. It took a great deal more than it took most men to get him to lose his temper. He seemed to know that when he did, he would unleash so much fury and rage, he couldn't depend on his power to rein it in. He was truly someone who was afraid of himself, of what he could or would do.

Amazingly, Mama never seemed afraid of him, never hesitated or stepped back even when it looked like she was treading on thin ice. I have seen her throw things at him, push him, even kick him. He was like a tree trunk, unmovable, untouched, steady and firm, which only seemed to get Mama angrier. Finally, frustrated with her inability to get the sort of reaction from him she wanted, she would retreat out of exhaustion.

"You're just like your father when it comes to your cold personality," she accused, pointing her long, right forefinger at me like some prosecutor—because to her way of thinking not to be outgoing and emotional was truly a crime. "There's where the ice comes into your veins. Certainly not from me, child. I'm full of heat," she bragged. "A man looks into these eyes and he melts."

She would wait for me to agree or smile or look like I was envious, but I didn't do any of that and that brought a sneer to her lips.

"What is with you, girl? You think you're better than everyone around here or something?"

I shook my head vigorously.

"Because I never did anything to make you believe that. I never pumped you up with compliments and such until you walked around with your head back, looking like you got flies in your nose or something, did I? Well, did I?"

I knew she would keep at me until I spoke.

"No, Mama."

"No, Mama," she mimicked. "So?" she said, her hands still on her hips, "why are you home all the time, huh? Why don't you have girlfriends and boyfriends? When I was your age, my daddy put a double lock on the door to keep the boys out. Here you are seventeen," she said, "and you ain't been out on a real date yet. I don't hear the phone ringing either," she complained.

It nearly made me smile to hear her grievances. All the other girls my age were constantly moaning and groaning about how their parents came down on them for being on the phone too much or being out too late and hanging around with bad kids.

"Are you ashamed of this place, ashamed of us? Is that why you hardly ever utter a word? Your family embarrass you? Huh?"

I shook my head again.

"Because the worst kind of girl is a snob girl," Mama declared. "She's worse than the other kind who teases and such. Are you a snob? Is that what your friends think, too? You think because you have a nice singing voice, you can't waste it on us ordinary folks? Is that it? Because if it is, that's a snob. Well? Answer me, damn it."

"I'm not a snob, Mama," I insisted. "I'm not ashamed of you or Daddy either."

Tears tried to come into my eyes, but I slammed the door shut on them.

She raised her eyebrows, surprised she had gotten so strong a verbal reaction from me.

"No? Well, what are you then? What's your problem, girl? Why do people talk about you being strange and mute? People here say good morning and you just nod or they ask you how you are and how your family is and you smile instead of talk. I hear about it. Some of them like rubbing it into me like oil or something. Is that why you don't have a close girl-friend and no boyfriends? I bet it is," she said nodding. "I know boys don't want to waste their time on someone who acts deaf and dumb.

"You ain't ugly, far from that, child. You look too much like me. What is it then? You just shy? Is that it? Was that grade-school teacher right about you years ago? You're Miss Bashful?" She drew close enough to me that I could smell the whiskey on her breath. "Huh? You got no self-confidence?" She poked me in the shoulder. "You afraid they going to laugh at you?" She poked me again. "Well?"

I put my hand over my shoulder where it was getting sore, but I didn't cry or even grimace.

"What?" she screamed at me.

"No one interests me yet," I said calmly.

That stopped her. She thought about it a moment and then shook her head.

"Well, you don't have to think of every boy as your future husband, Ice. Don't you just want to go out and have a good time once in a while?"

I didn't answer.

"You're shy," she decided, nodding firmly. "You're just too much like your daddy. He was so shy, I had to kiss him that first time. How's that? It surprise you to know that big, strong, bull of a man was afraid to kiss a girl? That's right. He was shaking in his shoes so bad, I could have pushed him over with one finger," she said, smiling. "I have that effect on most men. And you could, too, if you'd just listen to me. You don't even put on lipstick unless I hound you, and you still ain't trimmed those eyebrows the way I taught you."

Mama had spent six months in a beauty school when she was seventeen. It was her one real attempt at any sort of career for herself, but she lacked the sense of responsibility and the discipline to follow through. If she woke up tired, she just didn't go in, and soon they asked her to leave. However, she had learned a great deal.

"You need the arch," she pursued, running her forefinger over my left brow. "You put the high point directly above the middle of your iris. Brows are the frames of your eyes, Ice. Don't be afraid to tweeze them! Why should you be afraid of something like that anyway?"

"I'm not afraid, Mama," I said stepping back.

"Well then, why don't you do it? You can make your eyes look bigger. Remember what I told you: tweeze the hairs from underneath, not from above. Best time is after a shower. It's less painful, but a little pain can go a big way."

I looked down, hoping she would get bored as usual and start on some other pet peeve of hers, like how small our apartment was or how she couldn't buy the new dress she wanted because it was too expensive. Usually, she ended up threatening to go get a job, but she had yet to apply for work anywhere. Most of her day was spent looking after her hair and her skin, doing her beauty exercises or meeting her friends for lunch, which usually ran most of the afternoon. She always had too much to drink at those lunches and always reeked of smoke.

I once asked her why she smoked and drank if she cared so much about her looks and she responded by throwing a water glass across the room and accusing me of being too religious. She threatened to keep me from attending the church choir or make me quit the school chorus.

"It's the only time I ever see you show any interest in anything. What kind of a young life is that? Even birds do more than just sing."

Actually, both our school chorus and the church choir were award winning and were often asked to sing at government and charity events, but what did Mama know about that? She rarely came to hear me sing.

"You'll end up mealymouthed and fat, worrying about your everlasting soul day in and day out instead of having any fun," she rattled on. Now that she was on a roll, she seemed driven by her own momentum like some car that had lost its brakes going downhill.

"My mama was like that and that's why I was glad to get out of that house when your daddy came along and made me pregnant," she said without the slightest shame.

Other mothers would hide the fact that you were

an accident, but not mine. Depending on her mood when she talked about it, she was either seduced by Daddy or clever enough to get herself pregnant and married as a means of escaping imprisonment at home. Whatever the reasons, however, my birth had been a blow to her youth and beauty. She never stopped reminding me about that added inch on her hips besides the strain it was on her to care for a baby.

"If you looked after yourself more, you'd have boys asking you out, Ice. As it is, they won't give you a second look unless you become one of them easy conquests."

Her eyes widened with her own imaginings: me on a street corner or in the back of some parked car.

"You do that and I'll throw you out on the street," she threatened. "I'm not having people talk dirt about a daughter of mine."

I stared at her as if she was really talking non-sense now.

"Don't look at me like that, girl. It doesn't take much to turn a nice girl into a street tramp these days. I see it going on all around us. That Edith Merton might as well put a sign on her door out there," she declared, pumping her finger at our front door. "That whole family oughta be evicted."

The Mertons lived at the end of the hall. Edith's father was a city bus driver. She had a ten-year-old brother and her mother worked in a dry-cleaning and laundry shop. Edith's double trouble was to have developed a heavy bosom at age thirteen and to have parents who were so busy working to keep a roof over their heads and food in their mouths that she was left on her own too much.

Mama's obsession with herself and her youthful looks had one good result, I suppose. She was terrified of disease, especially anything that affected her complexion. I was prohibited from ever going into Edith's apartment, and I was never to invite her into ours. Mama saw her as walking contamination and pointed to every blotch on her face as evidence of some sexually transmitted disease.

As a result of what I learned people would call a bad neurosis, Mama wanted our home to be immaculate. If she did any real work, it was to keep our house and our clothing clean. Of course, I was the one who did a major part of all that, but I didn't complain. Except for my singing in the church choir and the school chorus and doing homework, I had little to compete for my time.

However, shortly after Mama and I had our most recent one-sided conversation about my anemic social life, Mama came to the conclusion that it was finally beginning to reflect poorly on her.

"I go out with my girlfriends," she complained, "and before long they're all talking about their kids in some new romance, bragging about the way they get all spruced up or how pretty they are and I got to sit there with my mouth as sewn tight as yours usually is, just listening and hoping no one's going to ask me about you. But I know what they're thinking when they look at me: 'poor Lena. She got that great burden to bear at home.' How do you think that makes me feel, huh?" she whined.

"I'll tell you," she said knowing I wasn't going to offer any answer. "It makes me feel like I got some kind of a retard at home, a girl who never gets her hair fixed in a beauty shop, never listens to me about her makeup, never asks for a new dress, never does nothing but read or listen to her music and go singing with some travel agents to heaven. You're an embarrassment!" she declared finally. "And I mean to do something about it once and for all."

I had no idea what she meant, but I did look at her with curiosity, which made her smile.

"You need a push, girl. That's all. Just a little head start. Even your daddy says so," she told me.

I doubted that. More than likely, she went into one of her tirades when he had just come home from work late and was tired and he couldn't offer much resistence. To shut her up, he probably nodded a lot, grunted and looked like he agreed, but my guess was he wouldn't even remember the topic of conversation the next day if he was asked about it.

At least, I hoped that was true. Daddy never lied to me or ever criticized me for being too quiet or too withdrawn. He liked the tranquility he and I enjoyed when Mama wasn't around to lecture us on one failing or another. More often than not, he and I would sit quietly, both of us reading or listening to his jazz records. We said more to each other in those silences than most people did talking for hours and hours.

"Listen to that trumpet," he would say and I would; he would nod and look at me and see that I understood why he loved jazz so much.

He had a valuable collection of old jazz albums that included Louis Armstrong, Lionel Hampton, Art Blakey on drums, and female vocalists like Carmen McRae, Ella Fitzgerald and Billie Holiday. He loved how I could listen to Carmen McRae singing "Bye Bye Blackbird" and then imitate her. He said I did a wonderful job imitating Ella Fitzgerald's "Lullaby of Birdland." He would play it and I would sing along. I could see the deep pleasure in his face whenever I performed for him. If Mama was there, she would thumb through one of her beauty magazines and look up at me occasionally, torn between giving me a compliment and complaining about me being content at home with them or my disinterest in the music girls my age loved.

"You're turning her into some weird kid. She doesn't listen to hip-hop or any of the music kids her age listen to and it's because of you, Cameron," she would grumble.

"I'm just listening to real music," Daddy would reply. "And she enjoys it. What's wrong with that?"

"*Real* music," Mama muttered. "My idea of real

music is going somewhere to hear it and dance and have a good time, not sitting in your living room tapping your fingers on the side of an armchair."

They did go out on weekends occasionally, but Mama was never happy about the places Daddy took her. The people there were either too old or too calm or out of touch with what was really happening.

"You're not out in the world like I am," she would tell him. "You just don't know."

Daddy didn't argue. He drew his music around him like a curtain of steel and sat contented, as contented as someone soaking in a warm bath. I listened, sang, learned about tempo and beat, phrasing and rhythm while Mama pouted or went into her bedroom to turn on the television set very loud. Those nights, we drove silence out the window.

Finally, Mama really decided to do something about me, to take control of my destiny, just as she had threatened. She was back to that idea that some girls just needed a little push. Well, she was going to give me more than a little push. She was going to give me a firm shove.

She returned one afternoon, stepped into my bedroom while I was sprawled on my bed doing my math homework, and made an astonishing announcement.

"Thank your lucky stars, girl. I got you a date with a handsome young man."

"What?" I asked, turning.

"I got you a date for Saturday night. We got to go

out and buy you something decent to wear and then I have to help you get yourself togther, fix your hair, do your makeup. When you go out with someone, you represent me, too," she declared. "People gonna say that's Lena Goodman's daughter and by the time I'm finished fixing you up, people gonna say, 'I would have known anywhere that was Lena's girl, a girl that pretty has to be her daughter.' "

"What do you mean, a date?" I asked, my heart thudding like a fist on stone.

"I know you kids don't like to think of it as a date. Somehow the word became old-fashioned. You just what—'hang out with someone' nowadays?" She smirked and shook her head. "Well, to me a date's a date. The man picks you up, takes you somewhere nice, and pays for everything. That's still a date in my book."

"What man?" I asked, sitting up.

"Louella Carter's younger brother Shawn. He's gonna be home from boot camp on leave this week-end, and we arranged for you two to be together Saturday night. He's a very good-looking boy and a boy in the army is gonna be well mannered, too. I spoke with him on the phone myself and he was all, 'Yes ma'am' and 'No ma'am' and 'Thank you, ma'am.' "

"I'm not going out with someone I never met, Mama," I protested.

"Of course you are. Didn't you ever hear of something called blind dates? You either got your nose in your schoolbooks or your father's old record albums, but you must've heard of that."

"I don't like blind dates," I said.

"You've never been on one! You've never been on any date, blind or otherwise, so how can you say you don't like it, Ice?"

"I just know I don't," I said.

"Well, this time you're gonna make an effort to like something I do for you. I didn't just go looking for a date for you, you know. I screened a lot of young men first. Louella's a girlfriend of mine and her brother's got to be a good boy who won't take advantage of an innocent girl such as yourself. I'm not saying he won't want to kiss you and such, but you know when to stop."

She thought a moment.

"Don't you?" she asked. "I mean, you learned all about that stuff in school, right?"

I nodded.

"Good. Then it's all set."

"Nothing's set," I said.

She glared at me a moment and then she stepped farther into my room, her eyes heating over, her jaw tightening, her hands folding into small fists pressed firmly into her thighs as she hovered over me.

"I said it's set. You're going to get all dressed up and have a good time whether you like it or not, and you're going to make me proud and give me something to brag about when I'm with my girlfriends, hear? This is one Saturday night you're not going to be shut up in your room singing to yourself or out there with your father and me listening to his antique records."

"But—"

"No buts, Ice. I want you to make a good effort toward having a good time. Do it for me if not for yourself," she added in a softer tone, practically begging. Her face looked pained with the effort.

I stared at her a moment and then looked down.

"Well?"

"Okay, Mama," I said.

"Good. Good. You're going to be thanking me afterward," she predicted. "You should be grateful that you have a mother who knows how to dress up and look good, too. Other girls depend on their friends or something they see in a magazine and usually look pretty stupid. I'm right here, at your side, giving you the knowledge I have from real experience.

"First thing we got to do is get your hair cut right."

"What? No, Mama. I don't want to cut my hair," I moaned.

"Of course you do. You don't know it right now, maybe, but once you're in the shop and my personal beautician Dawn starts working on your mop, you'll be very happy about it," she practically ordered. "You can't just keep your hair brushed down all the time. It looks drab."

She reached out and touched my hair

"And it doesn't have the body and silky satin feel

it should. Men like to touch nice hair and see a woman whose face is framed right. You're not taking advantage of your good qualities, Ice. I've been after you for months to do something about this...this mess, well now we have a reason to do it and we will.

"After that, we'll go look for a dress. Maybe we'll take advantage of some of those discounts your father gets, discounts we don't use enough. You'll need some new shoes, too."

"I don't want to cut my hair, Mama."

"I already made your beauty parlor appointment. It's tomorrow at nine."

"Tomorrow at nine? But I'll be in school, Mama."

"Not tomorrow, you won't."

"But —"

"You don't ever miss a day, Ice. You can miss one and don't tell me you can't. I see some of the girls in your class hanging around here during the school day, pretending to be sick or something and having a good old time of it. No one comes around to check on them either. At least you have a good reason not to go."

"Getting your hair done is not a good reason to cut school, Mama."

"It is to me, especially when you don't ever go and get it done, and especially when you have an important occasion coming up," she insisted.

"Important occasion," I mumbled under my breath.

"Yes," she said wagging her head, "it is an important occasion. It's like what they call those debutante balls or something, a coming-out."

I started to smile and her face turned hard and cold.

"Are you laughing at me, Ice?"

"No, Mama."

"Don't you go showing your stuck-up face to me."

"I'm not being stuck-up. But Mama, this is not anything like a debutante ball."

"It is to me and it should and will be to you. Now that's it. You can thank me later," she added and left me stunned and anxious about what she had done.

It was almost like the old days when parents arranged the marriages their children would have. If any of my classmates found out what she had done, I would really be the object of ridicule, I thought. Knowing Mama's girlfriends, it wasn't hard to believe the gossip would fly.

"Ice's mother has to find her a date. She can't get one on her own," they would say. They'd tease me and ask if my mother could find them a date, too.

I've got to find a way to get myself out of this, I thought. I could go to Daddy, but if I went to him, it could become a big blowup between them and they had been having quite of few of those lately. The last thing I wanted to do was be the cause of another.

Maybe I could pretend to be sick, I thought.

No, she wouldn't go for that. She's so excited about this, she'd send me out with a temperature of a hundred and five and a face covered in measles.

Maybe Louella's brother wouldn't show up. Maybe he would change his mind. Maybe he wouldn't like being made to go out with a high-school girl on a blind date. Maybe...

Maybe you might just have a good time, another voice inside me said. Maybe you'll like him.

Just maybe, your mother might be right. Don't try to tell yourself you never dreamt of having a nice time with a really nice young man.

Yes, your mother might be right.

I'd soon know, I thought and settled back into the inevitability of what was to come like someone floating on a raft toward Niagara Falls.

# 2

---m---

# The Makeover

From the way Mama talked and behaved, anyone would have thought I really was being prepared for a debutante ball. She couldn't wait to tell my daddy when he came home from work that evening, a little after ten. When he worked the later shift, he would have a sandwich for dinner, but that was never enough for a man his size, so Mama would prepare leftovers for him if she was home when he returned. If she wasn't, I would come out of my room as soon as he was home and warm up his dinner.

"Ice has a date Saturday night," I heard her tell him at the table.

We had a small, separate dining room and a four-chair yellow Formica breakfast table in the kitchen. She served the late dinner in the kitchen, ostensibly because she didn't want to mess up a clean dining room just for a leftover dinner. It made no sense to me because she would have to clean up the kitchen again anyway.

Despite her complaints, our apartment was a good size for the rent we paid and Daddy was always pointing out that the building was rent-controlled and we wouldn't get as much for our money if we did what Mama wanted and looked for another place to live. He tried to make it nicer to please her. He had friends who laid carpet and put up wallpaper and got some very good deals at the mall. No matter what he did though, the place was still "a dump" to Mama.

"Date? What kind of date?" Daddy asked. I could hear the concern in his voice, which took me by surprise. He rarely asked me anything about my friends or any boys at school. He never pushed me to go to dances or asked me why I wasn't going out on weekends.

"A nice date," Mama said. "I arranged it myself," she boasted.

"You arranged it? What do you mean? How?"

"I arranged for Louella Carter's brother Shawn to take her out. He's an army boy on leave from boot camp."

"Army boy? What kind of an arrangement is that? What are you saying, she never met him?"

"Now you tell me, Cameron Goodman, how is she going to meet anyone shut up in this place listening to music with you on weekends and such, huh? You think there's some sort of billboard out there with her face on it, announcing Ice Goodman's here, come and ask her out?"

"This doesn't sound good to me," Daddy said, his voice ringing with alarm.

"Oh no? And why is that, Cameron? Huh? Why? Because I made it all happen?"

"It just doesn't sound like it will be good. Army boys are a different breed," he warned. "Don't forget I was an MP. I know what being shut up with other men does to them, especially a boy just released from boot camp."

"Well, this time it will be good," she insisted. "Louella's a very nice girlfriend and I'm sure her brother's a nice young man. Besides, what have you been doing to help that child be a normal girl, huh? Nothing. You're content just keeping her home listening to music. How she ever going to meet anyone and get married that way?"

"She's only seventeen and still in high school, Lena. It's not exactly a crisis."

"How old was I when you married me? Huh? Well?"

"It was different," Daddy said almost under his breath. "You were different."

"What's that supposed to mean? You think she's better than us?"

"No. That's not what I'm saying," he said, but he didn't say it firmly enough for her.

"Blowing that child's ego up to make her think she's the Virgin Mary or something, raving about her singing all the time. No one's ever going to be good enough for her. Maybe that's what you want, Cameron Goodman. Maybe you want to keep her at your side all your days. Her hair will grow gray alongside yours listening to music. It's unnatural, that's what it is."

"Stop it, Lena."

"She's going on a date. She's going to be a normal girl who talks. And she's going to make me proud. Come aboard or swim to shore, Cameron, but don't you dare say one word against it, hear? I'm warning you."

Daddy was quiet. He wasn't happy, but he retreated as he usually did. His lack of enthusiasm and his warnings, however, put even more steam into Mama. Now she had to prove she was right. She couldn't wait to get me up and out to the beauty parlor the next morning. She made such a production out of it, I was truly embarrassed when we arrived.

"Here she is!" she cried as soon as we stepped through the doorway.

All the women in chairs turned to look and every one of the beauticians stopped work. Dawn, a dirty blond no taller than my old grade-school teacher, Mrs. Waite, emerged from the rear of the shop and looked me over as if I was someone just brought to civilization.

39

"She's got potential," she declared. "I see what you were saying, Lena."

Mama swelled with pride.

"But we've got some work here," Dawn added cautiously as she circled me. Everyone else was still looking at me.

"Pretty girl," the woman in the first chair said.

"Tall, like a model," the man working on her commented.

Dawn fingered my hair. "You're really dry, girl," she said. "And doing a lot of shedding."

"I knew it," Mama said. "She just hasn't looked after herself right. I've been hounding her, but you know young people today. You can't tell them anything."

Dawn didn't respond. She kept circling me, which made me even more nervous.

"We have to shampoo and condition plenty," she said. "Add moisture."

"Exactly," Mama said nodding.

"What have you been using on your hair, hand soap?" Dawn asked me. Everyone laughed, even Mama.

I looked down, debating whether I would just turn and run out or stay.

"Well, let's get you in the chair and get started," Dawn said. "We'll make it right."

"Go on, Ice," Mama coached.

Reluctantly, I walked across the shop, past the

other chairs and women and got into the chair reserved for me. Dawn came around and started to prepare the sink for my shampoo.

"You use a blow-dryer too much," she began, "especially with your dry hair. Why don't you give your hair a break and put it in cornrows?"

"No," I said sharply.

One of the women who was having it done turned to look my way.

"It's not for me," I added and gave Mama a look that told her I would get up and leave if they didn't listen.

"Just suggesting," Dawn said. "What do you say we do a press and cut, Lena? I'd bring it to here," she said pinching my hair at my chin. Mama nodded. Dawn looked at my face and smiled. "You've really never been to a beauty shop before, huh?"

"Not because of me," Mama said.

"This is going to look great," Dawn told me. "I'm going to insert a full head of weave, apply styling mousse and set your hair with a flat iron, curling the front down and the back up. You'll see. Great," she said.

Mama stepped back, nodded at Dawn and they began. I closed my eyes like someone about to go into an operating room and tried to shut out all the talk and laughter by listening to Daddy's music replay in my head.

When it was finally over, Dawn turned me around and stood behind me as proud as any artist. I gazed at myself in the mirror, amazed at the difference in my appearance. Not only did I appear older and more sophisticated, but Mama was right: I did have most of her good facial features, maybe even better because of my stronger mouth and bigger eyes and more prominent cheekbones—features I had inherited from Daddy.

"Well?" Dawn said. "You haven't said a word all the time I've been working. What do you have to say now?"

"She loves it. Don't you, Ice?" Mama asked, her eyes pressuring me to respond positively.

I nodded.

"Yes, I think I do," I admitted.

Mama let out a trapped breath, and she and Dawn laughed. Mama really looked pleased and that made her face even softer and younger. Anger always aged her instantly, like a dark hand waved magically in front of her.

"Now we'll do her eyebrows and I'll get her straight on her makeup," she told Dawn. "We're off to get her a nice dress."

"Are you going to a prom or something?" Dawn asked me.

I looked at Mama.

"No, she's going on her first real date."

"First? You're kidding me, Lena Goodman."

"I wish I was," Mama said. "We've got a lot of time to make up."

Dawn raised her eyebrows, looked at me and nodded.

"I bet," she said. "And I bet she will," she added.

Everyone but me laughed.

"Okay," Dawn said, "I gave you the best cut I could. Remember, before you go to sleep every night, prepare your hair for its own beauty rest. Apply a small amount of the moisturizer your Mama just bought for you, and to stop hair breakage, don't wear no hair band. We have satin sleep caps, Lena. Maybe you oughta get one for her."

"Yes," Mama said. "Absolutely."

Mama was on a tear now, spirited by our success at the beauty parlor. We took a cab to the Gallery at Market East and to Drawbridge's Department Store where Daddy had a twenty-percent discount. When I saw the price of the clothes, I didn't think it mattered if he had a discount or not, but cost didn't matter to Mama. She wouldn't let a little thing like breaking our budget for a couple of months stand in her way.

"I don't want you wearing those granny clothes young girls parade around in these days. Most of them look like sacks from thrift shops. And those clodhoppers they wear...I swear it's like girls are ashamed to show what they got anymore, or else they don't have it and don't have anything to show."

I tried to explain styles and trends to Mama, but she wouldn't hear of it.

"What makes you look good is in style and what doesn't is out of style in my book," she said.

We wandered through the teen fashions unsuccessfully. Mama didn't like anything. I thought she would give up on Drawbridge's, but she decided to go into the adult section, and she stopped in front of a manikin wearing what was called a princess cut blouse and skirt. It was a black and silver polyester jacquard material with a floral pattern on the blouse and a modest leaf pattern on the skirt. Because of the curve-enhancing princess shape in front and back, Mama thought it was sexy and stylish.

When I stepped out of the fitting room, Mama and people around her looked impressed. Other customers paused to look at us, too. I was embarrassed by the attention.

"What a perfect fit and what a beautiful figure your daughter has, Mrs. Goodman. She could model for us," the saleswoman said. "She looks like she's in her early twenties."

"Her father will have to sit at the door with a shotgun, you buy her that dress," a woman just passing said to Mama.

Mama was bursting with pride, her eyes electric, her shoulders hoisted.

"That's the latest fashion, you say?" she asked the saleswoman.

"Yes ma'am. It just came in yesterday, matter of fact."

"We'll take it," Mama decided.

It was an expensive outfit because of its designer, but Mama was determined.

"Your father can pick up some overtime," she told me when I showed her the tag.

"I don't need anything this expensive, Mama."

"Of course you do," she said. "The better you look Saturday night, the nicer you'll be treated. He's not going to take you to any Denny's in this," she said laughing. "That's for sure."

"Maybe he can't afford to do anything else, Mama," I said. After all, I didn't know anything about him and Mama really didn't know much either.

"That doesn't matter," Mama said. "When a woman impresses a man, he doesn't think of budgets and bank accounts and what he can and can't afford. He just thinks about one thing: impressing her. I know men, honey. And before long now, you're going to know them too, know just what to expect.

"Your education is starting a little later than mine did, but you have the benefit of me," she decided, nodding. "Truth is, I wish I had me when I was younger. I didn't have an easy time of it. My mother thought sex was such a dirty word, she had me and my sister and brother thinking we had been born through some sort of pollination, you know, like flowers? It got sprinkled on her stomach and we got created."

I smirked at her attempt at a joke, but she laughed.

"I'm not being funny. All she knew was the birds and the bees and that's what bees do; don't they spread the pollen? Bet you didn't think I knew so much about science, huh?

"I got a lot of surprises up my sleeve, Ice."

Suddenly, I was afraid she was telling the truth.

My heart ticked like a time bomb as Saturday night drew closer. That night after we had done all our shopping, Mama made me put on the outfit we had bought so I could model for Daddy. First, she worked on my makeup. She sat me in front of her vanity table and stood behind me gazing at my face in the mirror, scrutinizing. She decided I needed a little eye shadow. I thought it was too much, but she claimed my eyes were my strongest feature and I should do all I could to make them stand out.

"You have a natural pout," she told me, and decided to enhance it by dabbing a sliver of lip gloss onto the center of my lower lip. She showed me a trick to prevent lipstick from getting on my teeth. I was to put my finger in my mouth and close my lips. When I withdrew my finger, it removed any excess color.

"Someone once told me a beautiful woman's face was like an artist's palette. The artist sees the picture there and brings it out. You got to do the same with your face, Ice. Make it a work of art. That's what I do," she said softly, but with deep feeling.

I remember looking up at her and thinking with

surprise that she had more depth to her than I had ever imagined. Looking at myself in the mirror and at her behind me, standing there so proudly, I realized my mama had nothing but her good looks to rely on to give her meaning and purpose in life. Most of her girlfriends did look at her enviously and wanted to be in her company because her beauty had a way of spreading to them, embracing them, keeping them under wing. People, especially men, looked their way because Mama strolled along in the center. Maybe with the right management and some lucky breaks Mama could have been a model. As she sat there night after night, thumbing through those beauty magazines and gazing at the women who advertised beauty products or fashions, she had to be tantalized, taunted and frustrated knowing how much more beautiful and special she was.

It was funny how all this came to me in those moments before her vanity mirror. We had never had a real mother-daughter conversation about such things. Through the endless flow of complaints and moans she voiced in our small world, I was burdened with the task of understanding what she really meant and really felt. I had to read between all those crooked lines until I suddenly realized who she was.

Mama was a beautiful flower that had been plucked too early and placed in the confines of some vase where it finished blossoming and then battled time and age to keep from losing its special blush.

Now she was looking at me and thinking I would complete her, I would do all that she had been unable to do and be all that she had dreamed she would be.

"Children are our true redemption," the minister told us all one Sunday. "We believe they will redeem us for failing to be all that we had hoped to be, that they will do what we dreamed we should do and be whom we thought we should be. That's a healthy thing. 'Go forth and multiply,' " he recited.

The burden of such responsibility was heavy and something I didn't want, but I didn't have the hardness in me to turn around and say, "All this is your world, Mama, not mine. I don't need to be in the spotlight. I don't mind being in the chorus. It's the music that matters most."

Of course, I kept my famously shut-tight mouth zipped.

"All right," she declared when we were finished. "Put on your dress. Let's show your father how blind he's been by treating you like a little girl."

I was almost as nervous dressing for Daddy as I was to be dressing for Shawn on Saturday. Mama came into my room to make sure I had everything right. She had bought me a pair of shoes to complete the outfit and had given me her precious pieces of jewelry to wear: her pearl necklace on a gold chain with the matching pearl earrings.

"Turn down that music, Cameron Goodman," she

cried from my doorway, "and get yourself ready for a real surprise."

I felt like I was a runway model when I crossed from my room to the living room. Daddy obeyed Mama's command, turning down his music, and then she brought me into the living room. When he looked up from his big cushioned chair, his eyes did a dance of their own, enlarging, brightening, blinking and then suddenly narrowing with a kind of dark veil of sadness. I could see it clearly in his face. It was as if his thoughts were being scrolled over his forehead in big white letters: *My little girl is gone and in her place is this beautiful young woman who is sure to be plucked like her mother and taken off to be planted in someone else's garden. All I will have are the memories.*

"Well?" Mama demanded. "Don't just sit there acting mute too, Cameron Goodman. Say something. I spent a lot of time and energy on all this."

"She's...absolutely beautiful, Lena."

"You like the outfit?"

"Yeah," he said nodding emphatically.

"Good. You're going to need to remember that when you see the bill."

His smile froze, but he didn't show any anger or displeasure.

"She reminds me a lot of you, Lena, when I first set eyes on you," Daddy said.

Mama absolutely glowed.

"Told you," she whispered and squeezed my hand.

"She's prettier than I was, Cameron. I didn't know anything about hair and makeup then."

"You were a natural."

"There's no such thing. Every woman needs to have her good qualities highlighted," Mama insisted.

Daddy sat back, his smile warming again. Then he drew a serious expression from his thoughts.

"Where's this Shawn taking her?" he asked.

"How I am supposed to know? The man isn't here, is he? And when he comes, I don't want you treating him like one of your suspects or something."

"I don't have suspects," Daddy said. "Besides, there's nothing wrong in knowing your daughter's whereabouts when she goes out."

"I'm warning you," Mama replied. "I went through a lot of trouble to make this night special for her. Don't do anything to mess that up or I'll heave your precious old records out the window."

Daddy's face turned ashen for a moment and then he forced a laugh, shook his head and put up his hands.

"Yes, boss," he said and gazed at me. "I want you to have a good time, honey. I do."

I didn't say anything. My heart was doing too many flip-flops and there was a lump in my throat big enough to choke a horse.

Mama returned to my room with me to watch me put my new things away. She mumbled about Daddy not appreciating her efforts enough but blamed it on his being a man.

"Men expect too much and appreciate too little," she lectured. "They think you go into your room, fiddle about for a while and then come out looking like a million dollars. If you're taking too long, they moan and groan, but if you didn't look your best, they'd be unhappy because they wouldn't get all the congratulatory slaps on the back from their jealous friends.

"Men tell you they don't want other men gawking at you, but believe me, Ice, that's exactly what they want. It's like everything else they own. They want to drive a fancy car so everyone will look at them and be jealous. They want expensive watches and rings to draw green eyes. It's the same with their women."

I guess my eyebrows were scrunched. She stopped talking and smirked.

"You don't believe me, do you? What? You don't think men think of women as another possession? You still living in your books, girl. Forget all that romantic slop. What I'm telling you is the truth, is reality. You're going to start learning about the real world now and you'll come back to me and say, 'Mama, you were right. Tell me more so I know how to deal with it all out there.'

"That's what you'll be doing," she said nodding to herself and hanging up my skirt and blouse. "And I'll have lots more to tell you, too, more than you could ever learn from books and music."

She turned to me and looked thoughtful, looked on the verge of a decision. She made it quickly.

"Your daddy isn't the only man I've been with, Ice. I can see in your face that the news surprises, even hurts you, but a daughter becomes a woman when she can sit with her mama and hear about her mama's love life without squirming and hating her for it."

She was quiet. Maybe she was waiting for me to say I was ready, but I wasn't and maybe never would be.

"Don't worry," she concluded. "I'll know when it's the right time to tell you more about the real world."

She started out and stopped in the doorway, smiling.

"I wish I could be invisible, like one of them tiny angels, and ride on your shoulder tomorrow night and whisper advice in your ear when you need it.

"But you'll be fine," she decided. "You're my daughter. You got to have inherited something more than my good looks. Just don't be afraid to have some fun," she advised. She looked angry. "Don't be listening to those church choir songs in your head either. Last thing any man wants is to be holding hands with a saint or someone who's there to remind him he's headed for everlasting Hell just because he thinks you're pretty and wants to kiss you.

"If you got to sing anything, sing something lively," she said and left.

Poor Mama, I thought. She thinks this is all one big movie or musical.

And the irony was she thought she was getting me prepared for the real world.

Maybe there was no real world. Maybe it was all makeup and lights and curtains opening and closing.

And when you fell off the stage, that was when you were really dead or forgotten. No applause, no music, nothing but the silences so many people seemed to fear.

# 3

—*m*—

# The Kit-Kat Club

In my mind, Saturday morning began with a drum-roll. The moment the light slipped in around my window curtains to caress my face and nudge my eyelids open, it started. I had dreamt I was in the circus and Mama was the ringmaster, snapping her whip at the lions and tigers and drawing the audience's attention to the small circle in the center where I stood spotlighted in my new outfit, all dressed up and ready for "The Greatest Date on Earth."

As if she had been aware of my dreams, Mama swept into my room almost immediately after I had woken and had started to rise.

"I don't want you doing all that much today, Ice. You need to rest and do a beauty treatment."

"What's that?"

"You'll see," she promised.

After breakfast, Mama set out her creams and lotions. I never realized all that she had and did to herself before she ventured out in public. She had products to reduce tension, soften the skin, relax the eyes. She had creams for her hands, her feet. Later in the day she had me lie on the bed with slices of cucumber over my eyes.

Daddy was annoyed and disappointed because he received a phone call early in the day from his boss asking him to come in to work. He was supposed to be off, but his replacement had called in sick. Now he was worried because he wouldn't be home to greet Shawn when he arrived to pick me up. He wondered aloud if he shouldn't call to get someone to substitute for him so he could be here. Mama insisted it was unnecessary.

"I think I know the right things to say, Cameron, and besides, what's your being here going to do, huh?"

"I have enough experience to know what to look for in a soldier, Lena."

"Oh stop. You'll frighten the girl with that kind of talk and that's no way for her to be on a first date with someone. You need a can opener to get words out of her mouth as it is. If you keep up this talk, you'll put stress in her face," she added, "and ruin all my work."

"She didn't need all that work to start with," Daddy muttered.

Mama glared at him for a long moment. I thought it was going to turn into one of their bad fights, her eyes heating and brightening with her riled temper. She looked ready to heave something at him. Daddy glanced at me and quickly walked away.

"See what I mean about men?" Mama said nodding in his direction.

Actually, I was hoping Daddy would meet Shawn and I was more disappointed than he was, but I was concerned about making any sort of comment about it because Mama would feel I didn't trust her enough to do and say all the right things. She was so excited all day and hovered over me with reports from her girlfriend Louella telling her when Shawn would arrive, what he looked like when he did, and how much he was looking forward to this date, too.

"He's very excited about meeting you," Mama came by to tell me late in the afternoon. I was lying on my bed with those cucumber slices over my eyes, feeling very silly. "Louella said he's more excited about you than he is about seeing his family."

I took off the slices and sat up.

"How can that be, Mama? He doesn't know anything about me, even what I look like?" I asked.

She shifted her eyes guiltily away.

"Mama?"

"Well, I told Louella stuff about you and I gave her a picture to send him."

"What picture?" I asked.

"That one we took a month or so ago when we celebrated my birthday. I just cut me and your father out of the picture and sent you."

"I guess this is only a blind date for me then," I said.

"It doesn't matter, Ice. Any date with any new man is a blind date, no matter what people tell you about him. Believe me about that. If you hear about a man from another woman, it's half lies or exaggerations, and if another man tells you about him, you got to color in green for jealousy. There's only one person who can tell you what you got to know about a man and that's you."

She smiled.

"Maybe I oughta be writing a newspaper column of advice for lovers, huh?"

I widened my eyes and she laughed.

Nothing I could recall in our recent history made Mama so young, bright and happy as my impending date. I was afraid to utter one negative comment or iota of hesitation.

Before Daddy left for work, he stopped by and just stood in my doorway.

"I hope you have a good time," he said, "but if for any reason you're not happy out there, you don't hesitate to demand to be taken home, Ice. You make it clear and sharp, just like the orders he's growing used to in the army. Men need to be made straight right off. That's all I'll say," he added, "and that you're looking mighty pretty."

"Thank you, Daddy."

He nodded, kissed me quickly on the cheek and left.

Mama came rushing in immediately afterward.

"What that man say to you, Ice? He say anything to make you afraid?"

"No Mama. He just wished me a good time."

"Umm," she said still full of suspicion.

I looked at the clock.

"Getting about that time," she said. I really did feel like someone preparing for an opening, a big performance. "You dress in my room, use my table and stuff," she told me.

She hovered over me, making sure I put on the makeup she wanted as she wanted it, fixing every strand of my hair and then fussing over my new outfit. When I was completely dressed and ready, she surprised me by bringing out her camera and taking a picture.

"I want one of you and Shawn, too," she said.

"Oh Mama, it's going to embarrass him."

"Nonsense. Any man would want his picture taken with you, Ice," she said.

I wondered if she was right. Was I really as pretty as she was, and was it only because of my reputation of not talking very much that boys avoided pursuing me?

Exactly at seven, the door buzzer rang. I thought it stopped my heart. Then I heard the pounding in my ears. I tried to swallow, but couldn't.

Mama had gotten herself pretty dolled up, too, putting on her V-necked red dress and her pumps.

She strutted from her room, glanced at me waiting in the living room, smiled and went to the door.

"Evening, ma'am," I heard a deep, strong voice say. "I'm Shawn Carter, Louella's brother."

"Aren't you though?" Mama said. "And look how handsome in your uniform."

"Thank you, ma'am."

"Come right in. Ice is waiting for you in the living room, Shawn."

I felt my whole body tighten, my ribs feeling as if they were closing like claws around my insides. Mama came in first and then stepped aside to let Shawn enter. He stood there with his hat in his hand, gaping at me. For a moment neither of us spoke. I gulped a view of him and digested it.

He was about my height with broad shoulders, almost as broad as Daddy's, but he was nowhere nearly as handsome. He looked almost bald because of how closely his hair had been cropped and how far up his forehead his hairline sat. The close haircut emphasized his large ears. All of his features were big except for his eyes, which were small, beady ebony marbles. His lower lip was a little thicker than his upper and his jawbone was emphatic. His smile softened his initial appearance, however. It made him look younger.

"Hi," he said.

I was far from stuck-up, but a little voice inside me whispered: "No wonder he was so excited about taking you out, girl. You're probably the prettiest girl he's ever been able to date. Without the army uniform, he would be so ordinary you wouldn't give him a second look and maybe not even a first." Mama didn't really think he was so handsome, I concluded, unless she was bedazzled by a uniform. However, I was the first to agree that a book shouldn't be judged on its cover. It took time to learn if someone was truly handsome or beautiful inside.

Mama looked at me, her head bobbing, urging me to speak.

"Hi," I said.

"You look very, very pretty," he said. "Much prettier than you are in that picture my sister sent me."

"Bad camera lighting," Mama said. "Ice is very photogenic most of the time."

"Oh, she don't look bad in the picture," he quickly corrected. "She just looks a helluva lot better in person."

His smile widened and Mama laughed.

"Of course she does. Well, have a seat, Shawn and tell us a little about yourself before you two head on out. Unless you have a deadline to meet for dinner."

He nodded.

"Well, I was hoping we'd meet up with some of my buddies and all go to the Kit-Kat," he said.

"Oh. I don't believe I heard of that place," Mama said.

"It's a restaurant that has a jazz band," he told her.

"Jazz? Well now, Ice will appreciate that, I'm sure. Her father and her are jazz-a-holics," Mama offered and laughed.

"Jazz-a- what?"

"Never mind, never mind. Well, I won't keep you then," she said. "Ice, you'll need my light coat," she told me. We had already decided I would, but Mama pretended it was a last-minute decision. "I'll just get it for you. Pardon me," she told Shawn.

"Yes, ma'am."

"Oh, I just love that polite talk, don't you, Ice?"

Shawn smiled and looked at me. Mama waited for me to say something and then sucked in her breath with disappointment and went for the coat.

"Your mother's real nice," Shawn said.

I stood up.

"You know my sister?" he asked.

I shook my head and muttered, "Not really."

He nodded. His struggle to find the right words, or any words, was clearly visible on his face, especially in his eyes. He didn't want to look at me unless he had something to say. He kept his gaze low, nodding slightly as if his head was on a spring.

"You're in the twelfth grade, a high-school senior?" he asked.

I nodded.

"You look older," he said and then quickly added, "not old, just older."

I stared at him, wondering how he could have ever thought I'd think he meant old.

"Here we are," Mama cried bringing me her coat. She held it out and Shawn practically lunged to take it from her and help me on with it. Mama stood by beaming her approval.

"Oh wait," she cried. "Before you put that on her, I want a picture of you two."

I raised my eyes toward the ceiling.

"Fine with me," Shawn said. "Put me down for two copies. One goes right on my locker at the barracks."

Mama laughed and picked up her camera that she had placed on a table in the living room in anticipation.

"Just stand over there," she nodded a bit to our right. "Go on and put your arm around her, Shawn. She won't break," Mama advised.

I closed my eyes and bit down on my lower lip. His arm went over my shoulder and his big hand closed on my upper arm, pulling me closer to him.

"You can smile better than that, honey," Mama said. "Shawn here has a nice smile."

I forced my lips to turn and curl and she snapped the photo.

"One more," she said. "Just in case."

When that was over, I stepped forward out of Shawn's embrace and reached again for Mama's coat. He hurried to help me on with it.

"Well, thank you, Mrs. Goodman," Shawn said. "I'll show her a good time."

"I'm sure you will, Shawn. Don't be too late now," Mama called as we headed for the door.

"No ma'am," Shawn replied, but what did that mean? What was too late? Daddy would have been more definite, I thought.

"Have a really good time, Ice, honey," Mama called before the door closed behind us.

"We will," Shawn promised. He looked at me. "Okay, let's go burn up the town, huh?"

I started for the elevator and he took my hand. He grabbed it so quickly and firmly, he startled me for a moment. Then he pushed the button for the elevator.

"You grow up here?" he asked as the door opened. I nodded.

"Me too. I didn't finish high school, though. I decided to take that program the army has where you finish your diploma while you're in the service. I got started late in school," he explained. "My mother traveled around a lot with us before she settled in Philly. When I was fourteen, she took off with some computer salesman and left Louella and me. Louella had already gotten a good job so we were able to take care of ourselves," he continued.

As the elevator descended, he seemed determined not to let a moment of silence occur.

"I asked my sister how come your mother named you Ice and she said it was because you're a cool cat. Is that true?" he asked.

"No," I said and stepped into the lobby.

"Well, why'd she call you that then?"

I shrugged and he opened the front door. It was colder than I had expected. I closed the coat and held the collar tightly shut, waiting for him to direct me to his car. All I saw at the curb was a pickup truck with a cab over the back. I turned to him.

"I borrowed my friend Chipper's truck. My sister doesn't have a car and I haven't gotten around to getting one of my own yet."

We walked to the truck and he opened the door for me. When I got in, I smelled what I was sure was whiskey. The seat was torn in the middle and looked very ratty. I hoped there was nothing on it that would stain my new outfit. I saw a wrench on the floor and had to push it out of my way with my feet. He got in and started the engine.

"Here we go," he said. When he pulled from the curb, an empty beer can came rolling out from under the seat.

"Chipper ain't much of a housekeeper," he told me. "So, you ever hear of the Kit-Kat?"

I shook my head.

"They'll be checking IDs at the door," he said.

"I'm only seventeen."

"That's all right. Don't worry. We know the guy doing it. He's a friend of mine's brother. Besides, you look at least twenty. There's cigarettes in the glove compartment if you want one," he added nodding at it.

I shook my head.

"You don't smoke? That's good. I only smoke once in a while. Cigarettes, that is," he added laughing. "So, I bet you go out a lot, huh?"

I didn't know whether to tell him the truth or not. If I did, he would probably assume he was important and I knew instinctively that I didn't want him thinking that.

"A girl like you has to be popular. Not only are you good-looking but, from what Louella tells me, you're a singer, too. Where did you do your singing so far?"

"Chorus," I said.

"Chorus? That's it?" He laughed. "Hell, I was in chorus, too, but I'd never call me a singer."

He kept talking, describing his experiences at boot camp, the new friends he had made, the drill instructor he hated, and where he hoped he would be stationed someday.

Finally, he turned to me and smiled.

"My sister warned me you don't talk much. Why is that, if you have such a nice voice?"

"I talk when I have something to say," I told him.

He laughed.

"You'd fit right in at boot camp. My instructor is always shouting, 'Keep your hole closed unless I tell you to open it.' He gave Dickie Stieglitz KP for a week because he was mumbling complaints under his breath when we were in formation. The guy has radar for ears or something. He don't even have to be nearby to hear you.

"Hey, I'm going to get hoarse in the throat doing all the talking. Can't you tell me anything about yourself?"

"I like jazz," I offered.

"Great. Great. We're going to have a good old time of it. What's your drink?" he asked when we parked in a lot across from the nightclub. "Vodka? Gin? Beer?"

I shook my head.

"Bourbon, rye, what?"

"I don't drink," I said.

"Sure you don't," he replied with a laugh. "Hey, don't worry. I don't tell my sister about my dates, if that's what's troubling you. Your mother's not going to know anything from these lips," he promised.

I didn't say anything, so he opened his door and got out. Now that we were away from Mama's eyes, he didn't come around to open my door for me. Gone were the "Yes, ma'ams" and "No, ma'ams," too, I noticed.

When we stepped into the club, his friend checking IDs looked me over from head to toe, nodding with a smile so sly and licentious he made me feel naked.

"Nice," he told Shawn. "You're late," he continued. "Everyone got here already in your party."

"We'll make up for it," Shawn told him and ushered me into the club.

Right off the entrance to the right was a long bar

with tinsel over the mirrors that made it look like Christmas. The stools were all occupied and the bartender was so busy, he could barely raise his head. I noticed that the men were dressed well, jackets and ties, and most of the women were wearing expensive-looking clothes, too.

On a small stage, a five piece jazz combo played a Duke Ellington number I recognized. Shawn led me down the aisle to a table in the front at which three other young men in army uniforms sat with three girls—all looked years older than I was. The moment the men saw us, they started shouting and laughing, which I thought was impolite, considering people around them were enjoying the music. Of course, that drew a great deal of attention to us, especially to me.

"Where the hell you been? We thought you went AWOL on us," the tall, red-headed young man on the right cried. The girl with him looked unhappy, almost in pain. She had very short, dark hair and a mouth so soft, the lower lip looked like it was unhinged in the corners.

"Had to do the please-the-parent-thing first," Shawn explained. "This here's Ice. Ice meet Michael," he said nodding at the tall, red-headed man, "Buzzy," he added pointing to a stocky African-American man who looked older than everyone else, "and Sonny," he continued. Sonny looked the youngest. He had a caramel complexion with dark freckles peppered on his cheeks and forehead.

They all said, "Hi," and then Michael introduced the other girls. The one with him was Jeanie and the one with Buzzy was Bernice. She was stout and big busted with light brown hair that not only was the color of straw, but looked like it had the texture of it as well.

He paused before introducing the girl with Sonny and said, "What was your name again, honey?"

"I'm Dolores," she said, very annoyed that he didn't remember. She looked Latin, maybe Mexican. I thought she was the prettiest of the three because of the dazzling color of her dark eyes that flashed when she showed her temper. She got over it quickly, however, and continued moving in her chair, enjoying the music. "When are we going to stop all this talking and dance?" she cried.

"Sonny, get up and dance with the girl, will you?" Michael said. "Her engine's been running at high speed all this time and you're in park."

They all laughed.

Shawn took my coat off and put it over my chair. All of his friends stared at me as hard as the one at the club's entrance. It made me wonder if I had done something wrong. Mama had insisted on my wearing one of those wonder bras. I know I was showing a lot more cleavage than I would have liked.

I sat and Shawn quickly ordered a gin and tonic for himself and then looked at me and said, "Give her the same."

I didn't say no, but I thought I wouldn't drink it if I didn't like it.

"Why are you called Ice?" Buzzy asked leaning over the table. "You don't look cold to me."

They all laughed again, even Jeanie who seemed incapable of smiling.

"She's not cold," Shawn said. "She's cool."

"Ice, you can dip your finger in my drink anytime," Sonny quipped. They all laughed again.

"How long you know this work of art?" Michael asked me indicating Shawn.

I thought a moment.

"Twenty minutes," I replied and he roared and told everyone else what I had said. That seemed to be the funniest thing they had heard their whole lives. I thought the laughter wouldn't end.

The music stopped and the audience applauded. Our drinks came and Shawn nearly finished his in a single gulp.

"I needed that," he said. "Meeting a mother always makes me thirsty."

"I bet you've met a few," Buzzy said. "Are you from Philly?" he asked me.

I nodded. There was so much noise in the club, you had to shout to be heard and I knew what that would do to my throat in short order.

"You know how dangerous this guy is that you're with?" Michael kidded.

I shrugged.

"His life story is X-rated."

"You're right," Buzzy said after more laughter. "She's cool. She doesn't look a bit worried, Shawn. In fact, I think you'd better start worrying."

The music began again.

"You like this music, Ice?" Sonny asked, grimacing.

"She loves it," Shawn said. "She's a jazz-a-holic."

"Sure," Michael said. "You know this one?" he asked nodding at the band.

I smiled.

"It's a Benny Goodman tune," I said. They all turned to me. "Called 'After Awhile.' It's about 1929," I told them. Their mouths opened, jaws dropped.

"She's kidding, right?" Buzzy asked Shawn.

He shook his head.

"Her mother said she's into it and guess what," he added, "she sings, too."

"No. All this and talented too?" Michael cried. The other girls looked annoyed at the attention I was getting. Dolores finally got Sonny to get up and dance and then Shawn asked me if I would like to dance. I smiled to myself, remembering some of the steps Daddy had taught me.

I nodded and we got up. Shawn had no rhythm and couldn't do much more than pretend, but I ignored him, closed my eyes and let the music into me. I didn't realize how I was stealing the attention of the entire audience until the music ended and people applauded, looking more at me than they did the band.

The leader, a tall black man with gray temples and friendly eyes, smiled.

When we returned to our table, the boys were all raving about me and the girls were looking much more annoyed. Shawn ordered another drink for himself. I had just taken a sip of mine.

"C'mon, drink up," he urged. "We've got a lot of night ahead of us."

More reason to drink slowly, I thought, but everyone was ordering another drink by now.

We danced some more. Dolores tried to capture more attention with some very sexy moves. When Sonny asked me to dance, she looked like she would leap over the table to scratch out my eyes.

"Go on, give him a thrill," Shawn told me.

"I'd rather not," I said as gently as I could.

It seemed to take the laughter from all their eyes. When everyone was drinking and being silly, there was no room for any serious thoughts, I realized. It put a damper on things.

"That's being cold," Michael told Sonny. "Now I see the ice."

"Hey, give her a rest," Buzzy said. "Besides, it's time she sang."

I shook my head.

"No," I said.

He didn't listen. He jumped up and went to the bandleader, who looked my way and nodded. Buzzy beckoned to me.

"Go on," Shawn urged. "Show them a thing or two."

"No," I said shaking my head. People in the audience were all looking at me.

"What's the matter, this crowd's not good enough for you?" Jeanie asked me.

I looked at her.

"I never sang a solo," I said, hoping that would be enough.

"Tonight's the night you do," Michael declared.

Shawn started to help me up.

I shook my head again.

People were clapping on the right, urging me to get up. I continued to shake my head, but by now they were all cheering at our table, the girls the loudest, hoping I would make a total fool of myself.

For once, I thought Mama had named me correctly. My blood seemed to freeze in my body. I was numb with fear. And then, suddenly, I heard a familiar voice behind me.

"Go on, Ice."

I turned to see Balwin Noble, the senior at school who played piano accompaniments for our chorus.

"Balwin! What are you doing here?" I cried.

"I thought you said she doesn't talk," Sonny shouted at Shawn.

"I come here often and play with Barry Jones. Do 'Lullaby of Birdland,' " he urged. Occasionally, when no one else was at the rehearsal yet, he and I would fool around and I'd sing. Like Daddy, he loved my rendition of Ella Fitzgerald's hit song. "I'll get on piano."

"Really?"

"Who the hell is this?" Shawn demanded.

"I play piano for the school chorus," he told him.

"Well, this ain't school, stupid."

"I won't go up unless Balwin can," I declared.

The audience was getting impatient. People were clanking silverware against their glasses. Shawn looked around.

"Let him go," Michael said. "What do you care?"

Shawn stepped aside and Balwin and I walked to the small stage. They all did know him. The piano player got up to let Balwin take his place.

"Hey, Balwin," the bandleader said, "you sure about her? This isn't an easy crowd tonight."

"She's in the chorus. She makes it," he bragged. Then he leaned over and said, "C'mon, let's show them." He turned to the bandleader. "Do 'Lullaby,' " he told him.

"You've got it."

My heart wasn't pounding. It was clamoring, raging like a caged beast in my chest. The only thing that gave me some comfort was seeing Balwin at the piano. His familiar face and smile gave me encouragement.

"Wipe the doubt off their smug faces," he said.

I was given the microphone. Buzzy took his

seat. My table all gaped at me, the girls looking furious. Then the music started, I thought about Daddy and me in the living room and his happy smile and I began; soon, I wasn't in the Kit-Kat, I was back home. I was safe, and the song kept me safe.

When I finished, the audience was on its feet; even the girls at my table reluctantly stood to clap.

"Come around any time you want," the bandleader told me.

Balwin looked so proud.

"I knew you could do it," he said.

"I wouldn't have if you weren't here, Balwin."

"I'm glad I was," he said.

Shawn stepped up between us quickly.

"Nice," he said. "Really nice. C'mon. We're all going to Michael's house to party and celebrate."

"What? Why? What's wrong with staying here?"

"We're finished here," Shawn said.

I looked at the group getting up from the table and I thought about my father's advice.

"I don't want to go to anyone's house, Shawn," I said firmly.

"Why not?"

"We were supposed to go out to dinner. We haven't even eaten yet."

"We'll get something to eat there," he said.

"Maybe you should just take me home," I told him.

"Are you kidding?"

I shook my head and the smile of incredulity turned to a look of annoyance.

"Why?"

"I don't want to go to anyone's house," I said.

"I thought we were going to have a good time. Don't you want to have a good time?"

"Yes, but I don't want to go to anyone's house for it," I said.

"Aw, c'mon."

"No," I said as firmly as I could.

He glared angrily at me for a moment. Then he went to his friends to tell them, and they all started on me.

"We were just going to listen to music, have something to eat, enjoy the night."

"We can really party."

"What's the problem?"

I didn't reply to any of them. I sat at the table, my arms crossed under my breasts, fixing my attention on the stage and ignoring their comments and pleas.

"You got yourself a chunk of ice all right," Sonny told Shawn.

He stared down at me furiously.

"I'm leaving and going to Michael's," he finally said. "You coming or not?"

I looked up at him.

"No means no," I said as hotly and as firmly as I could. He snapped his head back as if I had slapped him across the face.

"Fine. Then let the fat boy take you home," he cried and turned away from me. "Next time my sister wants to fix me up with someone, I'll tell her to think twice. Go call *your* sister, Delores," he told her. "I should have listened to you and taken her out. This one's jailbait anyway."

All the girls laughed. I glared back at them and then turned away.

"Hey," Buzzy said leaning over to whisper in my ear. "You ever want to go out with a real man, call me. I'm in the yellow pages under Real Man."

He laughed and they all walked up the aisle, leaving me sitting by myself at the table. I was sure everyone around us was staring at me. Whenever I lifted my eyes from the table and turned, I met someone else's. I felt so stupid and frightened, very much an adolescent drowning in the world of adult quicksand. But I didn't move.

"What happened?" Balwin rushed over to ask me as soon as they all had left the club.

I told him quickly.

"How could he just leave you like this?"

I didn't reply. I stared at the table, my whole body still trembling. I felt his hand touch my shoulder gently.

"Hey, don't worry, Ice. I got my mother to give me the car tonight. I'll take you home," he said. "Do you want to go home?"

I nodded.

"I heard you say you haven't eaten. How about we stop for some pizza on the way? I'm hungry too. I'm always hungry," he confessed.

"Okay," I said. I would have agreed to anything to get out of here.

But as I rose to walk out the door with Balwin, I thought about Mama.

She was surely going to hate me.

# 4

## Allies

I decided not to tell Mama. Both she and Daddy were watching television when I arrived. I tried to be very quiet about it, but the moment I opened the door, Mama was up and in the living room doorway.

"Where's Shawn?" she asked looking past me. "Didn't he escort you to the door?"

I shook my head.

"Doesn't surprise me," Daddy called from the living room.

"And that doesn't surprise me," Mama shot back. She threw a suspicious glance at me and said, "Well, come in and tell us how it was."

"Fine," I said.

"Fine? That's it? Fine?"

Daddy looked up at me.

"I heard he took you to the Kit-Kat. They got Barry Jones playing there, right?"

I nodded.

"See, Lena, you didn't want to go there when I asked you to go last month, and here Ice goes and has a good time. Talented combo. What did they do?"

"Ellington, some Benny Goodman, a good Miles Davis," I recited. Daddy's eyes lit up.

"Oh, that you can talk about in detail, but when I ask you a question, I get 'fine.' What's all this talk about the music? What about Shawn Carter?"

"What do you expect her to tell you about him after only one time?" Daddy asked.

Mama shook her head at him and turned to me.

"Did you have a good time with him?"

I shrugged. "It was all right."

"Doesn't sound anything like a nice time to me," she muttered. "Ellington, Goodman, Miles Davis, they had a better time. Did you meet his friends? How were they? Did you make any new friends? Are you going out with him again?"

"Why don't you give her a chance to answer one question before you ask her another?" Daddy said.

"I'm waiting for her to say something that tells me something, anything, Cameron, thank you. I put in a lot of work for this and we spent a lot of money to get her out of this cocoon she's wrapped herself in, no thanks to you."

"They were all older girls, Mama. I don't think

they want to be friends with me. I'm still in high school."

"You don't look like a high-school girl, Ice. They should want to be friends with you. I bet you were the prettiest one there, right? Huh?"

"You're embarrassing her, Lena."

"She oughta be proud of herself and of me and what we did together. You can brag a little, Ice. Well?"

"I suppose I was, Mama." I looked at Daddy. "I sang 'Lullaby.'"

"You did what?" Daddy was almost up and out of his chair. "No kidding? With Barry Jones?"

I nodded.

"How did it go?"

"They all stood up and clapped," I said.

"You hear that, Lena? They all stood up and clapped."

"And what was Shawn Carter doing when this was going on?" Mama asked.

"Listening and clapping, too, I suppose," Daddy replied for me.

I nodded.

Mama narrowed her eyes.

"What kind of a date was this? You sang with the band?" she wondered aloud.

"She had a good time, Lena. Leave it at that."

"I'm tired," I said. "Good night."

"All she talked about was the music," Mama

moaned behind me. "When I went out with a man, I had a lot more than that to say."

"I bet," Daddy quipped and she turned on him.

I shut my door on the bickering and let out a hotly held breath.

I was hoping it was over. Mama would stop asking questions and eventually the whole thing would fade away, but almost as soon as I entered the kitchen the next morning for breakfast, she was on me again. Daddy was still in bed.

"What kind of a dinner did you have? Was it expensive? I bet you had something to drink, huh? I bet they didn't even ask you for identification. Well?"

"Shawn ordered me a gin and tonic, and no one asked me to show them any identification, but I didn't drink any of it," I told her. I was still traveling on the truth.

"Men like to ply you with liquor, so they can soften you up a bit. It's no harm done as long as you play your cards right. I always pretended to be tipsy, but I always knew what was going on around me. The rest of them drank plenty, huh?"

I nodded.

"You and Shawn just stayed at the Kit-Kat all evening?"

"Yes," I said, but I looked away too soon.

"He wanted to take you somewhere else?"

I nodded.

"Where? Damn, girl, why do I have to pull every word out of you? Why don't you just tell me the whole story at once? You ever say two sentences together?"

"He wanted me to go to one of their houses for a party, but I said no."

"That so? Well, that's all right. He should respect you more for that. It was only your first date, after all. You did right. I'm sure he understands. He did, didn't he?" she asked.

Just as I was about to burst and tell her all of it, the phone rang. We both looked at it. Mama smiled and I picked up the receiver.

"Hi," I said with enthusiasm after I heard who it was.

"That Shawn?" Mama whispered, hovering over me.

I turned my back without answering. It wasn't Shawn; it was Balwin.

"No, it's all right. We're up," I told him.

"I got a phone call just five minutes ago," he said, his voice rife with excitement, "from Barry Jones. They just got in from the evening. After the Kit-Kat club, they go to another hip jazz joint and play until morning. Then they go for breakfast and after that, go home and sleep all day."

"What a life," I said.

"Musical vampires. Anyway, he wanted to call me before he forgot. He was impressed with you."

"Really?"

"Yeah, but someone else was, too, someone named Edmond Senetsky, an entertainment agent from New York who was there with a client, sitting in the back of the club. He heard you sing and asked Barry about you and Barry told him he didn't know you, but he knew someone who did. That was me, of course."

"Well... what does he want?"

"Barry said he told him that you should audition for his mother's performing arts school in New York."

"New York?"

"What about New York?" Mama asked from behind me. "He wants to take you to New York?"

I shook my head.

"Yes," Balwin said. "He said you should prepare a couple of numbers for the audition and he gave Barry his card for you to call to get the details. Barry read the telephone numbers to me. You want me to give them to you now?"

"No," I said emphatically.

"Why are you saying no? You can go," Mama coached from the sidelines. Again, I shook my head.

"Well, should I come over later with it? This is a big opportunity for you, Ice. At least, Barry thought so and he knows. I heard of this school too. If I wasn't already going to Juilliard, I might be considering it."

"Let me think about it."

"Sure. I'm home all day today. I don't know if I

ever told you, but I've been composing songs. My parents got me a piano and put it in the basement. It's nothing like a studio, but I can record quietly and no one bothers me down there. Boy, I'd love to have you try one of my songs," he said.

"Okay, thanks."

"I'm going to call Mr. Glenn to see what he knows about this school in New York," Balwin said, referring to our vocal instructor. "We'll get his opinion about it all."

"Right," I said. "Bye."

"Call me as soon as you can," he said quickly and I hung up.

"What was that all about?" Mama pounced.

I stood there, staring at the phone for a moment and then I turned to face her.

"It wasn't Shawn Carter, Mama. It was Balwin Noble."

"Who's Balwin Noble?"

"He's a boy at school, the one who plays piano accompaniments for our chorus. He's that good," I emphasized, but she didn't look impressed.

"So? What's he want? What was that about New York?"

"He was at the Kit-Kat Club last night when I was there with Shawn," I began.

"Who was?" I heard Daddy say as he came through the kitchen doorway. He scrubbed his hair with his dry hands, yawned and stretched and looked at us. "What's up, you two? You make so much noise, a dead man couldn't sleep."

"If we lived somewhere where the walls weren't made out of cellophane, we could have a conversation without waking each other up in here," Mama retorted.

"Well, what's all the talk?"

"I was just asking about her date, that's all," Mama said.

"Oh, that again," he said. He went for a cup of coffee.

"Yes, that again. Then there was this phone call for Ice and I'm asking about that now. Is all this okay with you or do I need special permission to talk to my own daughter?"

Daddy didn't respond. He drank some coffee and began to prepare himself some eggs. He made omelets better than Mama, but I was afraid ever to say so.

"You eat yet?" he asked me. I shook my head. "Lena, you want an omelet, too?"

"No, I don't want any omelet. Damn," Mama said frustrated. She sat looking stunned for a moment. I went to put up some toast. "What was I saying?" she muttered, squeezing her temples between her thumb and fingers. "Oh yeah, New York...what about this boy, Balwin? What's he want?"

I took a breath, turned to her and began.

"When I was singing last night, Balwin was playing the piano. He's a very talented musician and he goes to the Kit-Kat occasionally to sit in with Barry Jones."

"Wow," Daddy said. "He must be very talented to have them let him do that."

"He is, Daddy."

"Well, that's just wonderful for him," Mama said, "but what's it got to do with you?"

"Barry Jones called him this morning to tell him a New York entertainment agent was there and heard me sing and wanted me to audition for a school for the performing arts."

"No kidding?" Daddy said. "That's terrific."

"What's terrific about it? How she going to go to a school in New York? You know what kind of money that means," Mama practically shouted at him.

"Well, let's see about it first," Daddy said.

Mama stared at him. Her frustration had made her eyes bulge and whitened her lips. She looked at me with growing suspicion now.

"Who brought you home last night?" she asked. "Well?" she demanded when I hesitated.

"Balwin," I confessed.

"Thought so."

"What's this?" Daddy asked, turning from the stove. "What happened, Ice?"

"I told Mama they all wanted to go to someone's house for a private party and I refused to go. Shawn didn't understand, Mama, and he didn't respect me for saying no. He got belligerent and he left me there."

"He did what? I told you..." Daddy stammered.

"Oh, shut up, will you, and let the girl talk, finally," Mama said.

"They were drinking a lot and Shawn was too. We never even had any dinner."

"That's what I expected," Daddy said nodding.

"Oh, you *expected*. What are you, a fortune-teller now?"

Mama sat there fuming.

"You didn't act mute or nothing all night, did you?" she asked with accusation written all over her face. "You didn't make them all think you were stuck-up?"

"No, Mama. I talked when I had something to say and when they asked me questions, but the other girls didn't want to hear me talk."

"I bet," Daddy said. "What a mess you put her into!"

"Me? I did no such thing. I tried to get her out with people, to become someone. Don't you go making statements like that, Cameron Goodman."

"It wasn't Mama's fault, Daddy. There was no way for her to know what it would be like."

"A woman with all her worldly experience ought to have known better," Daddy muttered and returned to his eggs.

Mama took the plate on her table, lifted it above her head and smashed it at his feet. He jumped back instinctively, accidentally hitting the handle of the pan, which sent it sliding over the range and onto the floor, spilling our omelets. It was all over in a split second, but it was as if the roof had caved in on our apartment.

"Look what you've gone and made me do!" Daddy cried.

"I'm tired of you making remarks about my past as if I was some kind of street girl, Cameron. I've told you that a hundred times, and I especially don't appreciate it in front of our daughter.

"Now, you've gone and filled her head with so much nonsense about this music thing, she thinks she can run off to New York and be a show star or something. She goes out on a date and gets up on a stage. I bet Shawn felt stupid."

"Why? He should have been proud she was with him. He should have appreciated her more."

"A man likes his woman to give him all her attention, not flirt with some piano player."

"I didn't flirt with him, Mama. He's just a friend. He plays for us at school. He—"

"Oh, I heard all that. You went and showed them you were nothing but a high-school girl. All my work and all that expense down the drain," she moaned, rose, glared at Daddy once and then marched out of the kitchen.

I started to clean up.

"Don't worry about her," Daddy said. "She'll get over it. You did the right thing not going to that house party. You'd a been trapped with a bunch of drunks," he said. "She knows that, too. She's just...frustrated," he added and helped pick up the pieces of Mama's broken dish.

This was my fault, I thought.

I should have just insisted on not going out.

I should have stayed home and not tried to be Mama.

Balwin called again in the early afternoon to tell me he had spoken with Mr. Glenn and Mr. Glenn had told him the Senetsky School was so special only a half-dozen new students get in it a year.

"It's not just a school. You live there and she teaches you how to handle the entertainment world, how to behave, dress, act—everything. Her graduates are all in Broadway shows or in television and film. As soon as you graduate, her son becomes your agent, and he's a very successful agent. It's the closest thing to a guaranteed successful ride into show business, whether you act, sing, dance, play instruments, anything she thinks shows real talent. You've got to do this, Ice. You've just got to give it a shot. I'll help you," Balwin added.

"I don't know," I said still trembling from the battle Daddy and Mama had in the morning because of me. The house had become a tomb—no one speaking, no music, barely any movement. Daddy sat in the living room rereading the same newspaper and Mama was lying down, a wet cloth over her forehead, fuming. I was afraid to make a sound. I was practically whispering on the phone.

"Something wrong?" Balwin asked.

"No," I said quickly.

"Well, I know this sounds like short notice, but why don't you come on over and we'll tinker around with some possible pieces you could use."

I didn't respond.

"You know where I live, right?"

"No," I said.

He rattled off the address and then added directions.

"It's only about a ten-minute walk from where you are," he concluded.

Balwin lived in a nice neighborhood. I had been down that street before, but I didn't know anyone who lived there, until now.

The night before he had told me a lot about himself. His parents were both professionals. His father was an accountant and his mother was a dental hygienist. Like me, he was an only child. He was about twenty pounds or so overweight for his five foot ten inch frame, but he had a nice face with kind, intelligent black eyes and firm, straight lips. He was definitely the best-dressed boy in school and was often kidded about his wearing dress slacks and a nice shirt. They called him Mr. Noble, making "Mister" sound like a dirty word. Some of our teachers called him Mr. Noble, too, but they weren't teasing him.

They were showing him respect because he was a good student, polite and very ambitious.

"Okay," I decided quickly. "I'll be there."

"Great. This is going to be fun," he said and hung up before I could even think of changing my mind. It brought a smile to my face, which had become like a desert when it came to smiles these days.

I put on my jacket and called to Mama and Daddy from the doorway.

"I'm going out for a while," I shouted.

"Bring back a carton of milk," Mama screamed back at me.

"Okay," I said.

I knew they both assumed I was just going for my usual walk around the block or maybe past some of the stores to look in the windows.

It was a cool, gray day with some wind. Spring was having a hard time getting itself a foothold this year. Winter just seemed to be stubborn, refusing to be driven off. We had had flurries in early April and only one day more than seventy degrees. Today it was in the low fifties. People walked quickly, some regretted not wearing their heavier coats and hats. The weather made them angry, as angry as people who had been cheated and scammed by some con man or woman. In this case, the villain was Mother Nature who had offered a contract with the calendar and then broken it with northerly winds and heavy clouds.

I wore a light-blue sweater and skirt along with a pair of black buzzin' boots with three-and-a-half-inch heels. I liked feeling tall. I heard some catcalls and whistles from men in passing cars, but I kept my eyes forward. Once you look their way, they think you're showing some interest.

A gust of wind brought tears to my eyes as I quickly whipped around a corner and headed down Balwin's street. I was practically running now. When I got to his door and pressed the buzzer, he opened it so quickly, I had to wonder if he hadn't been waiting right in the entryway the whole time.

"Looks nasty," he said glancing at the way the wind had picked up some discarded paper and chased it up the gutter.

I took a deep breath and nodded.

He looked nervous and started to talk so quickly, I thought he would run out of breath.

"I should have taken my father up on the car offer. He put a dollar value on my weight, offering to deposit so much for every pound I lost. I was to be weighed every morning before he went to work and he was going to keep this big chart up in his home office, but I never cared if I had my own car or not and he withdrew the offer."

He smiled.

"Maybe eating was just more important. Sorry. I could have picked you up tonight if I had my own car. My father won't let me use his car, and they took my mother's car tonight, which was the car I used to take you home from the Kit-Kat. They went to New York to see a show and have dinner," he said finally pausing for a breath. "Let me take your coat and hang it up for you."

I was shivering, but I gave it to him and he put it in the hallway closet. Whenever I visited anyone who had his or her own house, I understood Mama's constant longing to get us into something better. Odors from whatever other people on your floor were cooking didn't permeate your home. Noise and clatter were practically nonexistent. You had a true sense of privacy.

Balwin's house was a little more than modest. His parents had decorated it well. The furniture looked new and expensive. It was all early American. There were thick area rugs, elegant coffee and side tables, interesting pole and table lamps and real oil paintings on the walls, not prints. A large, teardrop chandelier hung over the rich, cherrywood dining room table.

"You want anything warm to drink? I'll make you some coffee or tea, if you like."

"Tea," I said nodding.

"Milk or sugar or honey?"

"Honey."

"That's good. That's what singers should drink," he said smiling.

I followed him into the kitchen and gazed at the

modern appliances and the rich cabinets. When he ran water into a cup and immediately dipped in a tea bag, I gasped.

"You forgot to heat the water," I said.

He laughed.

"No, this faucet gives boiling water immediately."

"Really?" I took the mug and felt the heat around it.

"C'mon, I'll show you my studio," he said proudly and led me back through the hall to a door. We went down a short flight of stairs to a large room with light oak panelling and wall-to-wall coffee-colored Berber carpet. The piano was off to the left. On the right was a bar and a pool table, a built-in television set to the left of the bar, and a small sitting area consisting of a settee and two oversized chairs, one a full recliner.

Against the wall on shelves were neatly stacked tapes, records and CDs, below them was Balwin's sound system.

"These amplifiers are four hundred watts," he began, beaming with pride. "I've got multitrack recording capability with nonlinear track mixing and editing as well as digital mixing on this sixteen-track, twenty-four bit studio recording worksta-tion."

One look at my face brought a laugh to his.

"Sorry," he said. "I get carried away sometimes and talk the talk."

"I don't know much about these things."

"It's all right. The main thing I'm trying to say is we can produce a CD of your singing if we have to, but whatever we record, it will be very high quality. Just in case they ask for something like that."

"I don't have money for this, Balwin."

He laughed again.

"You don't need any money, Ice. I'm taking care of all that."

"Why?"

"Why?"

He looked flustered for a moment, glanced at his piano, and then smiled and said, "Because I love music and I love to hear it done well and you do it better than anyone at our school," he explained.

Embarrassed by his explanation, he moved quickly to the piano and scooped up some sheet music.

"Look these over. I sifted through my collection to pick out what I thought you might like to do and what you could do well," he said.

I put the mug of tea down on a small table and went through his suggestions. One brought a quick smile to my face. It was Daddy's favorite, "The Birth of the Blues." He loved Frank Sinatra's rendition. I pulled it out of the stack.

"What about this?" I asked.

He nodded.

"That's the one I would have chosen for you, too," Balwin said. "Let's tinker with it."

He went to the piano and began to play. I didn't need the sheet for it. I had sung it enough times, singing along with Daddy's Sinatra recording.

"Jump in any time you want," Balwin said.

I did. He played to the end and then nodded.

"Good," he said, "but you're going to do a lot better before we're done."

I laughed at his tone.

"You sound like Mr. Glenn talking to our chorus."

"I'll try to be for you," he replied. "Ready? We'll do it a few times, record it, listen to it and correct whatever we want to correct."

I smiled at him. The night before he had tried so hard to cheer me up after what had happened to me at the Kit-Kat Club. His first thought was that I was unhappy about not being able to please Shawn Carter. He wanted to know how long we had been going together; when I told him it had been my first and only time with Shawn, he looked relieved and surprised.

"I don't hang around with anyone in particular at school," he told me as he turned from the piano, "so I don't know about everyone's social life, but that was the first time I've seen you at the Kit-Kat. Where do you usually go on dates?"

"I don't," I told him.

"I don't understand," he said.

"I haven't gone on many dates."

The more he learned about me, the happier he became.

"Why are you smiling?" I finally asked him.

"You're a lot like me," he said. "All this time, I thought you were so quiet and reserved because you were so far ahead of everyone else at the school socially. That's why I wasn't surprised to see you with the army guys."

I looked at him quizzically. Was it just him or did others at my school think that of me?

"I mean," he quickly added, thinking he had somehow put me down, "you definitely could be in an instant, if that's what you wanted."

I laughed to myself. Why did everyone, including and especially Mama, think I was so special?

"I'm not trying to be above or ahead of anyone, Balwin," I told him.

He smiled and after a moment softly said, "You don't have to try, Ice."

Was he just trying to make me feel good again? Or was he saying these things because he was as much a loner as I was and I had come to his house? My guess was I was the first, the first girl at least.

Did he ask me because he really, truly believed in my talent or because I was a girl?

*Questions, doubts, suspicions.*

Why can't you just accept a compliment and leave it at that? I asked myself. What are you afraid of, Ice Goodman?

Being too much like your mother?

She would certainly ask the question.

Maybe, deep down inside, you're really afraid of not being enough like her?

Shut up and sing, I told myself. Just sing.

# A Song of My Own

I thought our first rehearsal went just all right, but Balwin was more enthusiastic. When he referred to me, he used words and expressions like "terrific," "amazing talent," "a prime candidate for any school." Of course, I assumed he was just being nice. I knew what it meant to compete in the world of entertainment. Daddy had told me lots of stories about singers and musicians he had known in his life, people who were talented and yet failed to get anywhere because they didn't have the breaks they needed or the grit to keep trying.

"It's much easier to accept failure and become comfortable with it than it is to keep coming at them, Ice," he said. "You blame it on destiny or fate or luck and just settle into mediocrity. Lots of good people I know lost the fire in their spirits and now smoulder in some dark, small place, drowning their ambitions and dreams in alcohol or drugs."

The way Daddy spoke about it made me wonder what had been his private dream. When he finally revealed that he had once hoped to play the trumpet because his teacher had encouraged him, I was surprised. He had never even hinted at it before. Then he dug down in a dresser drawer to show me his trumpet mouthpiece. His maternal grandmother had bought him the instrument.

"It's all I have of the trumpet I once had," he said. "I blow on it from time to time when I get nostalgic."

"What happened to your trumpet, Daddy?" I asked.

His eyes darkened and he shook his head.

"My father made me pawn it, only I pretended to have lost the mouthpiece. He beat me for that," he said.

"Why didn't you go back to playing, Daddy?" I asked him.

"I guess I was afraid," he said. "I was afraid I would get so I couldn't live without it and that would make it terrible, Ice."

I had never known my grandfather. He had died when I was only two, but if he was alive now, I wouldn't be able to look at him without hating him. Amazingly, Daddy didn't sound hateful or angry.

"Didn't you hate him?"

"No." He smiled. "He couldn't see how it mattered in my life then and the money was sure handy that month," Daddy said.

Hearing him speak about it made me wonder about all the secrets people buried in their hearts, all the dreams that had been crushed and interred. Those were the real silences, the ones they were afraid to disturb. It frightened me and did the most to make me hesitant when it came to my own singing and dreams of success. Dare I dream?

It was probably why I just shook my head at Balwin and thanked him for his compliments as if I knew he was doing it just to be nice. I could see the confusion and even the anger in his eyes.

"I mean it," he insisted. "You're going to make it, Ice. I love music too much to lie about something like that," he added.

"Okay," I said. "I'm sorry. Thank you."

We scheduled another rehearsal. As if he was afraid talking about it or even referring to it during the school day might put a hex on it or something, he actually avoided me. I quickly realized he was the shy one when it came to being with someone from the opposite sex. Like me, he used his music as both a shield and a way to communicate with others. Without it, he was almost as much a mute as I.

Even at chorus rehearsal, he didn't say anything special to me. When I said I would see him later, he nodded quickly and turned away, afraid someone nearby would notice.

Mama wasn't home for dinner. She had gone to a movie with two of her girlfriends. Daddy had another one of his late nights. I expected to be home before either of them, so I didn't leave a note telling them where I was.

Just as the first time, practically the instant I rang the doorbell, Balwin was there.

"Hi," he said and I stepped in. He looked nervous, jittery. Without another word he started for the doorway to the basement studio.

Just before we reached it, however, a tall, lean man with a patch of gray hair encircling his shiny bald head stepped into the living room doorway. He was holding a neatly folded copy of the *New York Times* and was dressed in a three-piece pin-striped gray suit and tie.

His lean, long face was as shiny as the top of his head. His skin was so smooth in the reflected hallway light, he looked like he shaved with one of Mama's tweezers. I saw a resemblance in his and Balwin's mouth and eyes and the shape of their ears.

"Who's this?" he asked sternly.

Balwin glanced at me as if he had smuggled me into his home and been caught in the act. I saw a look of abject terror take over his face, his eyes shifted guiltily away and down as his shoulders slumped and his head bowed slightly to make him look like a beaten puppy.

"Her name is Ice Goodman," he said almost too softly for even me to hear.

"Ice!"

Balwin raised his head and nodded.

"If you have a friend coming over, why don't you

tell your mother or me and why don't you make a proper introduction instead of stealing away to your bunker?"

"I wasn't stealing away. We were..."

"Well?" his father demanded.

Balwin stepped forward, glanced at me and then said, "This is my father, Mr. Noble. Dad, this is Ice Goodman, a girl from school who is in the chorus."

"I see. And you are here to do what?" he asked me.

"She's here for a rehearsal," Balwin said before I could reply.

His father glared at him and then turned back to me, his eyes narrowing.

"Rehearsal? Why would you rehearse with only one member of the chorus and why can't you do this sort of thing at your school?"

Although he was asking Balwin these questions, he continued to stare at me.

"It's not a chorus rehearsal," Balwin said.

"Oh?"

He turned to him.

"And what exactly is it then?"

"She's going to audition for a special school and needs to prepare some music. I'm helping her," Balwin explained.

"Is that so?" He looked at me again and then turned to Balwin. "Am I correct in assuming you've completed all your homework?"

"Yes sir," Balwin said.

"What school is holding this audition?" he asked me.

"She's auditioning for the Senetsky School in New York," Balwin replied quickly.

"I was asking her," his father said. "She's a singer, you say, but I have yet to hear her utter a sound."

"I was just—"

His father's glare was enough to snap Balwin's mouth shut. I had never seen such obedience coming from such terror.

"It's the Senetsky School," I repeated.

His father barely looked at me before turning back to Balwin.

"I see. Well, your mother has a bad headache this evening, so don't make your music loud," he ordered.

"Yes sir," Balwin said.

His father snapped the paper in his hands like a whip, turned and disappeared into the living room. I could see Balwin visibly release a trapped breath.

"C'mon," he said and continued to the stairway.

"I don't want to cause any trouble," I said before starting down.

"It's all right," Balwin said looking up at me. "My father doesn't think much of my music, my composing. He likes to recite statistics about how difficult it is to succeed in the creative arts. Everything I have here, I've bought with my own money, and money my mother gave me. Please close the door behind you," he added and continued down the stairs and to the piano.

I looked at the living room doorway and then stepped down and closed the basement door.

"When I sell something for a lot of money, my father will change his tune," Balwin muttered.

It was hard getting myself back into the spirit of singing. Every time I raised my voice, I thought about his father hearing me and becoming enraged. He wasn't half as wide or as powerful looking as my father, but there was something more terrifying about Balwin's father. His name should be Ice, I thought. Those eyes looked like they could stab someone with a sharp, hard glare.

"Don't be afraid to get into it," Balwin said after we had run through it twice. "My mother won't be able to hear you and even if she did, she wouldn't complain like he says."

"I don't want to get you into trouble."

"You won't," he insisted. "C'mon. I want to make a CD soon. You'll be able to play it for people."

We started again and I gave it more energy, which brought a smile back to his face.

"That's more like it," he said after we finished. He played the recording he had made and we listened and followed the music. "Right there you should give it more authority," he said, using one of Mr. Glenn's instructions for the chorus.

I smiled.

"Don't you agree?"

I nodded and he looked embarrassed. When the recording was finished, he asked if I would like something to drink.

"I can make tea down here. I've got a microwave behind the bar."

"Okay," I said and watched him do it. As he prepared a cup for himself and me, I walked around the basement, looking at the posters on the wall and some of the photographs in frames.

"Your mother's pretty," I said.

"She's gained a lot of weight since that picture," he told me. "I guess I take after her in that respect. Maybe in most respects," he added.

He put my cup of tea on the bar and I sat on a stool. He remained behind it, sipping from his mug and watching me mix in some honey.

"My father is so precise about everything he does, including eating. He's proud of the fact that he hasn't gained or lost a pound in twenty years. He once tried to starve me to make me lose some weight," Balwin revealed, shame in his face.

"Not really?" I said.

He nodded.

"I could only have a glass of apple juice for breakfast and then he had everything I ate for dinner weighed on a small scale. Of course I snuck candy bars and ate what I wanted at school. He actually searched my room the way someone might search it for drugs and found two Snickers bars and a box of malt balls. I love malt balls. He went into a rage and put a lock on my piano and threatened to sell every piece of equipment if I didn't lose five pounds that month.

"My mother was so upset and cried so much, I had to do it. Finally, he relented and took the lock off the piano. But I regained the weight the following month and he threw his hands up one night and told me he was giving up on me."

He looked away to hide the tears that had come into his eyes. When he turned back, he put on a smile quickly.

"It's all right. We've got a sort of fragile truce in the house now. At least he's happy about my grades. I guess he loves me. He's just one of those people who have a hard time revealing it. He thinks it's weak to show too much emotion. He came from a very poor family background and made a success of himself. He says no mature adult can blame failure on anyone but himself. There's always a way to get around an obstacle or solve a problem if you really, truly want to do it.

"I guess he's right."

He sipped some more tea and then shook his head.

"I'm sorry. I didn't mean to blab like that."

"It's okay," I said and smiled.

"You're cool, Ice. Sounds funny to say that, I know, but I can't imagine you blabbing. I bet you would have been great in silent movies."

I laughed.

"No, really. You say more with your face, with your eyes, than most of the girls do talking all day. I like that. The fact is," he said looking down, "I've written a song about you. I hope you don't mind."

"Me?"

He nodded.

"It's not that great."

"Where is it?"

"In here," he said pointing to his temple. "I haven't written it down yet. I'm still playing around with it."

"I want to hear it," I said.

He took a deep breath and looked almost as terrified as he had upstairs in front of his father.

"Please," I begged.

"If it sounds terrible, promise you'll tell me the truth, okay?"

I nodded.

He walked around the bar and went to his piano. I followed and stood by it, waiting. He glanced at me, looked up and then began his introduction. He sang:

*There is music in the silence of her smile.*
*There's a melody in her eyes.*
*She glides unheard through the clamor that's*
    *around her,*

*but it's in the harmony of her that beauty lies.*
*Listen to the patter in my heart; listen to the*
    *drums within my soul,*
*see how she can make the chorus sing and see*
    *how she can make the symphony start.*
*Play, play this song of you.*
*Play for the old and play it for the new.*
*Play at the break of day and play in the*
    *twilight hour.*
*Play away the sadness and the sorrow.*
*Walk before the saddest eyes you see.*
*Walk and bring the music back to me.*

He stopped and stared down at the piano keys.

"That's all I have so far."

He looked up.

It had been a long time, a very long time since anyone or anything had brought tears to my eyes, tears I couldn't hold back, tears with a mind of their own that surged forward and out, streaking down my cheeks; glorious tears, unashamed, proud to reveal that my heart was bursting and I had been moved.

"Well?" he asked.

I walked around the piano and answered him by kissing his cheek. He was so surprised, his eyes nearly popped. I had to laugh and flick away the tears from my cheeks.

"Thank you. It was beautiful," I said.

He beamed.

"It's not finished, like I said. I'll work on it every day. I'll have it perfect. I'll—"

"How long is this rehearsal, as you call it, to go on?" we heard and looked at the stairway where his father stood midway down.

How long had he been there? Had he seen and heard Balwin singing the song to me? Did he see me kiss him?

"We're just finishing up, sir," Balwin said.

"Good."

He turned and stomped back up and out, closing the door.

"Sorry," Balwin said. "He gets that way sometimes."

What's he afraid of? I wondered, looking after him.

"I've got to get home anyway. My father is coming home late and I have to get his supper. My mother's out with friends," I said.

"Okay. We'll meet again tomorrow night, if you want."

Balwin saw my eyes go to the upstairs doorway.

"It'll be okay," he added.

I nodded and started up the stairs. I was so quiet. Balwin's father didn't seem to mind silence. There was no sound of television, no music, just the heavy ticking of the grandfather clock in the hallway.

"Good night," I told him at the door. "Thanks."

I stepped out quickly. The wind greeted me with a slap in the face and cold fingers in and under my unzipped jacket. I quickly did it up and hoisted my shoulders for the walk home. Just before I reached the corner, I heard a car slow down and turned to see two young men looking out at me, one with a ski cap and the driver with a cowboy hat. The one with the ski cap wore sunglasses even though it was night. I recognized them as former students at my school. I was surprised they knew me.

"How about a ride, Ice baby?" he asked. "It's warm enough in here to melt you."

"Real warm," the driver shouted.

I kept walking, but they continued to follow.

"What's a pretty girl like you doing out here alone anyway?" the one with the sunglasses continued. "You and your boyfriend have a fight?"

I walked a little faster, my heart thumping and echoing in my ears like a pipe being tapped with a wrench in my building. Suddenly, just as I was about to turn the corner, they pulled ahead of me and the door swung open. The one with the sunglasses stepped out and made a sweeping bow and gesture toward the car.

"Your chariot awaits, m'lady."

I stopped, terrified.

"Ice!" I heard and turned to see Balwin running to catch up with me. He stopped, gasping for breath. "Sorry. I had to do something first," he said looking toward the car and the man with the sunglasses.

"Who's this? Balwin Noble? Can't be your boyfriend. He'd crush you," the man with the sunglasses said and laughed. His friend laughed, too.

"Forget it," the driver called to him.

"You missed out, honey," he told me and got into the car. We watched them drive off.

"I was watching out the front window and saw them slow down," Balwin said. "I'll walk you home."

I started to shake my head.

"I should have offered to anyway. My father gets me all wound up in knots sometimes. Sorry," he said and started. "C'mon," he urged.

We walked on together, Balwin with his hands deep in his pockets.

"I'm going to go on a diet tomorrow," he said. "Really."

I smiled to myself and we walked on, Balwin doing all the talking, me doing all the listening, but feeling good, feeling warm and protected.

We said good night in front of the apartment building and I thanked him.

"I'll ask my father for the car tomorrow. When he hears I'm going on a diet, he'll be nicer to me."

"Okay," I said. "But don't make any trouble on my account."

Balwin smiled.

"Can't think of a better reason for it," he said, leaned forward to give me a quick peck on the cheek and then turned and hurried away as if he had truly stolen a kiss.

\* \* \*

Daddy got home earlier than I had expected. He was already in the kitchen, sitting at the table, eating what he had warmed for himself. My look of surprise appeared to him to be a look of guilt and worry, I guess.

His eyebrows lifted and he peered suspiciously at me. "Where were you, Ice? You didn't go and meet that Shawn again, did you? Your Mama didn't go and make another one of her special arrangements, I hope."

I shook my head.

"So, where were you?"

"Rehearsing," I said and entered the kitchen. "Sorry I wasn't home to fix your dinner, Daddy."

"That's no bother. What do you mean, rehearsing? Rehearsing for what?"

I shrugged.

"C'mon, out with it," he said.

"I know I'm just wasting my time," I said.

"Ice, what is this? What are you talking about?" he asked slowly.

I lifted my gaze from the floor and looked at him.

"My audition piece for the New York school," I said quickly.

"Really?" He sat back nodding. "That's good, Ice. That's good. Where were you rehearsing?"

I told him about Balwin and how he was helping me.

"Very nice of him. I'm glad about this." He turned to me quickly. "And don't go saying you're wasting your time. I don't want to hear that defeatist stuff from you, hear?"

"But it will be too much money, won't it, Daddy?"

"You just let me worry about that when the time comes to worry about it, honey." He nodded. "We'll manage it somehow. I'm not going to let you miss such an opportunity, no sir, no ma'am."

I smiled to myself and started to clean the pot and the stove while he finished eating.

"Your mother say where she was going tonight?"

"Movies."

"Movies, huh? If she went to all the movies she says she went to, she'd be seeing stars and I don't mean the movie stars," he quipped.

He was trying to be funny, but I could see the concern in his face. It put a cold shiver in me.

"Can't make that woman happy anymore," he muttered, mostly to himself.

I saw how quickly his elated mood turned sour and dark. He stopped eating, stared blankly ahead for a moment and then rose and went into the living room to play one of his Billie Holiday albums while he waited for Mama to come home. After I finished in the kitchen, I went in to sit with him.

"You look tired, honey," he told me nearly an hour later. "Go on to bed. I'm all right by myself. Go on. Get some rest," he ordered. "You got school tomorrow."

I rose, kissed him on the cheek and went to bed. I couldn't fall asleep. I kept hoping I'd hear Mama's

footsteps in the corridor and then the front door opening, but an hour passed and then another and, still,
she wasn't home. This was going to be a very bad
night, I told myself. My stomach churned like a car
without fuel, grinding and dying repeatedly. I tossed
and turned and tried desperately to think of something else, to sing myself to sleep, anything. Nothing
worked.

When the front door finally opened, it was close to
three in the morning. Mama didn't just come in, either. It sounded like she fell in.

I sat up to listen and heard her muffled laugh. She
was very drunk.

"What are you doing on the floor, Lena?" I heard
Daddy ask her.

She laughed and then she told him the heel broke
on her shoe. I could hear her struggle to her feet, still
giggling to herself.

"Where were you all this time, Lena?"

"Out," she said. "Having a good time. Ever hear of
such a thing? Know what that is anymore? I doubt it,"
she told him.

"Where were you?" he repeated.

"I said out," she snapped back at him.

I heard him step forward and then I heard her short
scream.

I rose from bed and opened my door just enough
to see the two of them.

Daddy had his hands on her upper arms and he

was holding her up like a rag doll, her feet a good foot off the ground. He shook her once.

"Where were you, Lena?" he demanded.

"Put me down, damn you! Put me down."

"Where were you?"

"I'm not one of your suspects, Cameron. Put me down."

"I'll put you down," he threatened, "like they put down dogs if you don't tell me where you were."

"I was with Louella and Dedra. We went to eat and then we went to a movie and then we went to Frank and Bob's just like we always do."

Daddy lowered her slowly.

"I'm tired of you coming home drunk," he said.

"People drink because they're unhappy," she spit back at him.

"Why are you so unhappy? If you got yourself a job, maybe or…"

"Oh, a job. What kind of a job could I get, huh? You want me working in some department store or at a fast-food place?"

Her face crumpled as she started to sob.

"I wasted myself. I should be on a magazine cover or doing advertisements. I should be somebody instead of…of what I am," she moaned. "But do you care?" she asked, pulling herself up and tightening her lips. "No. You and your music and your stupid work hours."

"I'm doing my best for us and…"

"Best," she muttered. "You don't care about what's happening here. We got a daughter who's like some deaf-and-dumb person, who should be making me proud, and I blame that all on you, you!"

"She's a beautiful girl, a talented girl. She's going to make us proud, Lena."

"Right. I go and work on her and get her a date and it all falls apart."

"You know that wasn't her fault."

"I know. It was mine," she screamed at him. "Who else would you blame?"

"Nobody's blaming anybody, Lena."

"Leave me alone," she said. "I'm sick. I'm not feeling good."

"Why should you after what you did to yourself?"

"You did it to me," she accused.

"Me?"

"You made me pregnant when I was young and beautiful and had a chance, Cameron. And then you promised to do things for me, but look at what you've done...nothing. Nothing but tie a lead weight around my neck.

"I'm drowning!" she screamed at him. Then she seized her stomach, doubled over and hurried to the bathroom.

He stood there looking after her, his face as broken and sad as I had ever seen it. He felt my eyes and turned to my doorway.

We looked at each other.

Was I the weight Mama said was around her neck? Did he hate for me to have heard such a thing?

The pain in his eyes was too great for me to take.

I closed the door softly and returned to bed, to the darkness and to the pursuit of fugitive sleep.

# 6

---

# Out of Tune

There were many times when the mood and atmosphere in our house resembled an undertaker's parlor. I call it *morgue silence* because to me everyone who is infected with it seems to be imitating the dead. I've been to funerals where people sit in the presence of the corpse and keep their eyes so still and empty, I imagined they have just deposited the shell of their bodies in the funeral hall for a while and then have gone off to kill some time at some livelier place.

However, when the singing started, it was always like everyone had turned into Lazarus and risen from the grave. As a little girl, I was so impressed with the energy and the emotion some people exhibited at these wakes that I often wondered if they wouldn't revive the dead man or woman whose eyes would suddenly snap open and then sit up in the coffin and begin to join in the singing. Once, I imagined it so vividly, I thought it actually had happened. Mama saw me sitting there with my eyes so wide and full of amazement, it made her nervous. She insisted on taking me home because she thought the funeral was making me crazy.

"And she's crazy enough with her elective mutism," she told Daddy. She loved using that term ever since she had first heard Mrs. Waite use it at the parent-teacher conference.

Everyone was an elective mute in my home the morning after Mama's late night out. We had *morgue silence*. Mama didn't rise from her bed, but she wasn't asleep. I looked in and saw her staring up at the ceiling, her lips tightly drawn like a slash across her face. Daddy sipped his coffee and stared at the wall. I felt as if I had to tiptoe about the apartment, getting ready for school. He didn't say anything until I was ready to leave.

"I've got a double shift today," he told me. "Training two new men. I won't be back until late, but don't fix me any dinner. I'll have enough to eat this time," he said, his voice trembling with anger and disgust. "She might put poison in my food anyway," he muttered glaring in Mama's direction. "Blaming everyone but herself for her unhappiness."

"I can make you something, Daddy."

"No, it's all right," he said. "I might be later than usual. Don't worry about me," he ordered. He was wound so tight this morning, I was already feeling sorry for anyone who crossed him at work.

I nodded and finished my breakfast without another word and left for school.

The moment I arrived, I sensed something different. I knew from the way other students (especially some of the girls in my class) looked at me; hid smiles behind their fingers, spread like Japanese geisha-girl fans; or deposited whispers into each other's ears that I was once again the object of some ugly joke. Usually, having a thick skin came naturally to me. Whatever darts of ridicule they shot from their condescending eyes or spewed from their twisted, vicious lips bounced off the back of my neck and fell at their own feet like broken arrows. Most of the time, ignoring them as well as I did brought an end to their little games. They grew bored trying to get any sort of reaction from me, and when I looked at them with a blank stare, a face that could easily be lifted and used as a mask of indifference at a Stoic's convention, they retreated and searched for a more satisfying target.

Today was different because I could feel their determination and their satisfaction growing with every passing minute—from homeroom to my first class of the day—despite my apparent disinterest. I was confused by it and couldn't help being curious. Was it something my mother had done? Or had said? Were they all just learning about my blind date and laughing at the results? What could possibly be the reason for all this whispering and laughing behind my back? It followed me from room to room like a string of empty cans tied to some poor dog's tail. The faster I walked, the louder the whispering and laughter became. When I sat in my classes, I merely had to turn slightly to the right or the left to see all eyes were on me, girls and boys mumbling over desks, making such a thick underlying flow of chatter that our teachers had to reprimand them a number of times and threaten to keep the whole class after school.

Their persistence began to make me nervous, but I was able to keep the lid on my emotions, walk with my eyes focused straight ahead, behaving as if there was no one else in the world. Finally, just before lunch, Thelma Williams and Carla Thompson stepped in front of me as I walked to the cafeteria. They wore identical wry smiles and with their books in their arms, their shoulders touching, presented themselves like a wall thrown up to block my way.

"What?" I demanded when they continued to just stand there, grinning.

"We were wondering if you and your boyfriend Balwin would like to come to a party at Carla's house this weekend?" Thelma asked in a phony sweet tone of voice.

"What?"

"We've never invited you to anything because you never showed any interest in boys before," Carla said.

"Some of the girls were worried you might be gay, you know. They don't like undressing in front of you in the locker room," Thelma emphasized.

I shook my head and started to go around them.

"How long have you been secretly seeing Balwin?" Carla asked as they stepped to the right to keep me blocked.

I stared at them. Balwin? Could Balwin have said something to someone about me? It seemed unlikely.

A small crowd began to gather behind them.

"What we were wondering is how does he make love with that big belly of his in the way," Thelma said. The others were starting to giggle. "I told Carla you would always have to be on top, right?"

"You're disgusting," I said.

"There's nothing wrong about being on top," Carla said. "As long as there's something to be on top of."

That brought a loud laugh. Some boys passing nearby stopped to listen.

"I've got to go to lunch," I muttered and stepped forward again, but they didn't part to make room for me.

"Well, are you coming to the party or not?" Thelma asked. "We'll have Carla's bed reinforced to handle the extra weight."

She turned to the appreciative crowd and smiled before turning back to me.

I fixed my glare on her.

"You must be very sexually frustrated," I said. That drew a loud howl from the boys on the rim of the circle.

"Not so frustrated that I'd be going to Balwin Noble's house. You've got to find his thing with a tweezer."

Laughter rolled like thunder down the hallway and over me. My heart pounded. Rage rose in my blood.

"You've got that wrong, Thelma," I said so calmly I could have been talking about a problem in biology. "It's your brain that has to be found with a tweezer."

I forced my way between her and Carla as the boys roared with laughter, most of them now turning to tease Thelma. She cursed them. Before I made it to the cafeteria doors, I felt her books slam against my back. She had heaved them after me. They fell to the floor. I paused, took a deep breath and then just walked on, passing Mr. Denning, the cafeteria's teacher monitor, who nodded and smiled at me. He heard the commotion continuing outside and turned his attention to it, ordering the crowd to disperse.

They did, but shortly afterward, there was a great deal more noise in the hallway and Mr. Denning had to rush out again. A group of students gathered at the doors to watch and then everyone scattered to his table when three other teachers appeared.

What was going on now?

I was shaking in the lunch line and still trembling when I finally sat down with my tray of food. Arlene Martin and Betty Lipkowski, two white girls who had always been pleasant and friendly, were already seated at the table. They were in the chorus, too.

"I guess Mr. Glenn's going to be accompanying us on the piano today," Betty said.

"Why?" I asked.

"Didn't you see what was going on out there just now?" Arlene asked me.

"I saw enough out there," I muttered.

"Balwin got into a bad fight."

"What?"

"He and Joey Adamson had to be pulled apart by Mr. Denning. He took them both to the principal and you know fighting is an automatic three-day suspension, no matter who's to blame," Betty said.

"How does it feel?" Arlene asked.

I stared at her.

"What?"

"You know, to have a boy get into a fight over you?"

I looked down at my food. I had to keep swallowing to stop what I had already eaten from coming back up.

"Sick," I finally said.

"What?" Betty asked.

"Sick. It makes me sick," I said, rose and walked out of the cafeteria.

The remainder of the day passed in a blur. My teachers' voices ran into each other in my mind. I moved like a robot, unaware of how I went from one room to another. When Miss Huba called on me in my last class of the day, Business Math, I didn't even hear her. I guess I was staring so blankly and sitting so stiffly, I frightened her. She came to my desk and shook my shoulder.

"Ice? Are you all right?"

I gazed up at her, and then looked at the rest of the class. Everyone stared, all looking like they were holding their collective breath, waiting to see if I would scream or cry or laugh madly.

"Yes," I said softly. Her previous math question entered my brain as if it had been waiting at the door. I rattled off the answer. She smiled.

"That's correct. Okay, let's turn to the next chapter, class," she said.

When I looked at the others again, their expressions varied from amazement to disappointment. After Miss Huba made the assignment and gave the class the last ten minutes to begin, a silence thickened around me. Then, Thelma Williams, who sat in the last seat in the third row, loudly muttered, "Give her a tweezer." The whole class roared. Miss Huba looked up confused. And I...I felt as if each syllable of laughter was like a pebble thrown at my face.

Finally, I gave them what they wanted so desperately.

I covered my face with my hands, rose and ran from the classroom. Miss Huba's amazed voice was shut off by the door I slammed behind me.

I didn't go to chorus rehearsal. I went straight home. I was glad for once that Mama wasn't there to greet me. I dreaded her questions, her demands to know exactly why I had cut my chorus rehearsal, especially with the concert coming up in a little over a month. She would dig and scratch until she got all of it out of me.

Of course, I felt terrible. Balwin had only tried to do me a favor, had only tried to help me with my future and now found himself not only the target of ridicule, but in trouble at school, probably for the first time. I shivered thinking of what his father might do to him.

About an hour later, I heard Mama come home. She was mumbling to herself, not realizing I was already home. I let her go to her room and then I came out of mine, expecting to see her any moment and gearing myself up for her cross-examination. She didn't come out. I waited and waited and finally went to her door and peered in. She was in bed again and fast asleep with an opened bottle of aspirins on her night table. I decided it was best not to wake her.

When I started making some supper, I heard her call to me and I returned to her room. She had risen and gotten herself a cold washcloth, which she had over her forehead.

"This has been the worst hangover of my life," she moaned. "I'll never drink cheap gin again. Don't you ever do it, Ice. If you drink, insist your man buys you the best," she advised.

"I don't drink, Mama."

"Yeah, yeah, but you will someday," she insisted.

"Are you hungry?"

"Not with my stomach," she complained. "I tried to eat some lunch today and it nearly came up as soon as I swallowed. Just make me some coffee, will you, honey?" she asked.

I nodded and did so. I gave her a steaming mug of black coffee, which she sipped, closed her eyes, and sipped again. Then she looked up at me sharply.

"Where's your hardworking father?" she asked.

"He's doing a double shift today, Mama."

"Figures. The day I need him around here, he's baby-sitting some department store."

She dropped her head to the pillow as if her head was a solid chunk of granite and closed her eyes.

"Get me two more aspirins," she ordered.

After she swallowed them, she said she wanted to just sleep until next week.

I returned to the kitchen and continued making myself some supper. Before I sat down, however, there was a loud, strong knock on our front door. I listened and heard the knocking again.

"Yes?" I asked with the door closed.

"I'd like to speak to you, Miss Goodman," I heard. The voice was strangely familiar. I churned through my memory desperately, trying to recall where I had heard it before and then realized. It was Balwin's father!

I looked back toward Mama's room, waiting to hear her ask who it was, but she didn't call out to me.

"I'll just take up a few minutes of your time," I heard Balwin's father say.

With trembling fingers, I opened the door and stepped back to let him in.

He stood there gaping in at me. Dressed in his dark gray pin-striped three-piece suit and his tie with his gold cuff links visible, he looked almost as alien in this building as someone from outer space. His lips were pressed tightly shut, which drew the skin on his chin into a small fold.

"Thank you," he said stepping forward. He gazed around as he closed the door behind him, nodding softly as if what he saw confirmed what he believed and expected.

"What do you want, Mr. Noble?" I asked.

I had already made up my mind to stay away from Balwin and would agree to it immediately as soon as he demanded it. I expected to hear his complaint, how I had caused his perfect student son to misbehave seriously for the first time ever, proving I was a bad influence on him.

"I'm here to ask for a favor," he began, "but not a favor I expect to be gratis," he quickly added.

He gazed at the doorway to the living room.

"Are your parents at home?"

"My mother is, but she isn't feeling well and she is in bed," I said.

He nodded.

"Well, can we sit down for a moment?" he asked.

I led him into the living room. He looked over every possible seat as if he wanted to be sure to choose one that wouldn't leave a smudge on his immaculate suit. Our apartment was far from dirty. The furniture might look worn, but there wasn't any dust nor were there any stains. He chose to sit in Daddy's chair. I remained standing.

"Well, now," he began, his fingers touching at the tips, "I suppose you're aware of what went on today."

I nodded.

He tilted his head and almost smiled.

"I was obviously quite taken by surprise when I received the phone call from the principal. My Balwin? Fighting? I remember girls on the playground pushing and kicking him around and him not lifting a finger to defend himself—or even to voice a complaint, for that matter. I thought he was without any self-respect. Other children his age could wipe their shoes on him and he would stand there obediently as if he were a living rug. I can tell you how much that bothered me, and when he began to gain weight, I

thought it was just a logical consequence of the soft-
ness in his spine. He has no pride."

"That's not true," I cried.

He snapped his hands apart as if I had driven mine
through them.

"No," he said nodding, "I realize now that there
are some things that will motivate him to stand up for
himself, to care about his self-image and the image
he presents to others. One thing at least, I should
say," he concluded, gazing up at me and nodding.

I waited, my arms now wrapped around my body,
under my breasts.

"You know I'm referring to you. This fight today
was over you, as I understand it. He was defending
your honor. Of course, he received three days' suspension at just the wrong time of his high-school life,
when he's expected to do well on his exams and prepare to enter a prestigious institution. He's got his
heart set on this Juilliard, but I have gotten him to at
least apply to Yale and Harvard."

"Mr. Noble—" I began, but he put up his hand to
stop the traffic of my words.

"How, I asked myself, how can I take advantage of
this rather embarrassing situation so it won't be a
complete loss? I make my living doing that for others
in a sense, so I should be able to do it for myself,
don't you think?

"For the longest time, I have tried without much
success, to get Balwin to look at himself in the mirror

and see what everyone else sees. I have tried to explain, to demonstrate, to emphasize just how important appearance is in this world. People, for better or for worse, most often judge others on the basis of their looks, the image they present. Clothes do make the man, Miss Goodman, and so does your personal hygiene and your physical self.

"In Balwin's case it's deplorable. He has nice clothes to wear and he takes good care of his wardrobe, but you can't turn a pig into a swan merely by dressing it in pretty feathers."

"Balwin is not a pig," I blurted.

He stared at me and then closed his eyes for a moment, as if he had to seize control of his raging emotions.

"No," he said opening his eyes again. "He's not a pig in spirit even though someone looking at him might think he overindulges, as do pigs."

"What do you want from me?" I demanded, growing tired of listening to Balwin's father tearing him down.

"I want you to get him to lose weight," he said.

"What?"

"You heard me. I want you to get him to shape up, to improve his self-image. I know you can motivate him now because of what's happened. That shows some commitment to something other than his music.

"Of course, I don't expect you to do this without receiving some compensation so I am prepared to make this offer...I'll give you ten dollars for every pound you get him to shed from now until the end of the school year," he stated.

I simply stared at him.

"Twenty pounds gets you a quick two hundred dollars. I'm sure you could use it," he said, glancing around the living room. "No," he said after another moment of my silence and my famous penetrating stare, "I should improve this offer. Tell you what. I'll increase the dollars per pound with every five pounds so that pounds one to five, you'll get fifty dollars, but pounds six to ten, you'll get double that, a hundred dollars, and then pounds ten to fifteen, we'll make triple and quadruple the amount for fifteen to twenty. Anything more than twenty, I'll give you fifty dollars a pound. How's that sound?"

"Stupid," I said. "Insulting. Depressing, disgusting and insensitive," I concluded. "Balwin will lose weight when he wants to lose it and not because I tell him to lose it."

Mr. Noble smiled.

"Please, Miss Goodman. We both know that a boy who has a crush on a girl, as Balwin has on you, will do almost anything the girl asks him to do. All I'm asking is you...lead him on a bit. I don't have to tell you how to get a boy to do your bidding, I'm sure. Only this time, you can earn some good money for it.

"I might even be inclined to throw in a bonus if

you succeed in making a difference in a few months. It will be a nice graduation present and what harm will you have done? Nothing. But you will have helped Balwin immensely. Wouldn't you like to do something good for someone and make money doing that as well?"

"I don't need to be paid to do something good for someone," I said.

I heard Mama's distinct groan and looked toward her bedroom, expecting her to make an appearance and be shocked at the sight of Mr. Noble. It grew silent again, however, so I turned back to him.

"My mother's not well, Mr. Balwin. I'm sorry, but you should leave."

"Fine," he said, standing. "Think over my offer and get back to me. You can continue to come to the house to practice your music, of course, and benefit that way, too."

He walked to the front door, opened it, and stood there a moment.

"Don't be so quick to condemn a father for trying to help his son," he added and then slipped out gracefully, closing the door softly behind him.

I stood there for a moment staring after him. Then I heard Mama behind me. I turned and saw her shaking her head.

"I raised a fool," she said. "I heard all that. You just went and threw out hundreds of easy dollars."

"I couldn't take money from Balwin's father for

something like that, Mama. I'd feel like a traitor or something," I said and started for the kitchen.

"Why? Who you betraying? Some fat boy? Believe me, Ice, you don't get a chance to take advantage of men much in this world. It's usually the other way around. Think of that Shawn Carter. Didn't he try to take advantage of us? Of you? It just comes natural to men, so why shouldn't you benefit from an opportunity, huh?"

I started to shake my head.

"If you don't want the money, take it and give it to me, for godsakes."

"I can't, Mama," I said.

She smirked and nodded.

"Right, you can't. And what have you been doing over that boy's house anyway, huh? C'mon, tell me all of it."

"We've been practicing music for my audition," I revealed.

"Thought so. Your father know about this?"

"Yes," I admitted.

She pulled herself up.

"Well, that figures, too. Secrets. You and him keep secrets."

"No, Mama," I cried. "He didn't find out until last night when I came home. I would have told you, too, but you didn't come home until very late..."

"Sure, blame it on that. He blames everything on me, too," she said.

She took a deep breath, turned and went back to her bedroom. I wanted to follow her and explain more, but I thought she would only close her ears as tightly as she closed her eyes. Later, I tried to get her to eat something and she finally relented and had some toast and jam.

"You take that money," she told me when I brought it into her. "Don't be the fool I've been. Take whatever you can while you can. It doesn't last long. Before you know it, they're looking at younger women and you might as well be invisible," she complained.

I went to my room to finish my homework. Just before ten, Balwin called.

"I guess you heard what happened," he began.

"I'm sorry, Balwin. I never wanted to get you into any trouble," I told him.

"It's not your fault. Jeez, Ice, you can't blame yourself for what those idiots do. I shouldn't have let him get to me," he said, "but I wouldn't let him say those things about you."

"I know," I said. I wondered if he had any idea his father had been to my house. "Was your father very angry?" I asked.

"Not as angry as I expected he would be. He didn't even ask about the cause of the fight and he hasn't said a bad word about you, Ice. I don't mind the days off. I'll work on my music. I'll finish your song, too," he vowed.

"Balwin..."

"You'll come over after dinner tomorrow night, won't you? Please? I'll feel like a total idiot if you don't," he explained. "Like it's all been for nothing, a waste."

I smiled to myself.

"Are you sure, Balwin? It won't stop at school, you know."

"I know. I don't care. Matter of fact," he said, his voice deepening, "I think I'm going to start to enjoy it. They're just jealous, that's all.

"Here, the prettiest girl in the school and the most talented, too, is friends with me, coming to my house," he bragged. "I guess they just don't understand the power of music as well as we do, right, Ice?"

He waited.

"Right?"

"Right, Balwin," I said.

"Okay. Same time, okay?"

"All right, Balwin," I said.

"I can't think of anyone I would rather get in trouble over than you, Ice," he said. Then he quickly said, "Good night," and hung up.

It was just like before when I felt he had stolen a kiss.

It brought a deeper smile to my face.

Music is powerful, I thought. It can make you feel so much better about yourself and your life, it can help you visualize your dreams, it can give you hope and strength. Just like Daddy, Balwin and I would wrap our music about ourselves snugly and shut out the nasty world.

Let them curse and laugh, ridicule until they're blue in the face.

All we'll hear is the rhythm and the blues or the melody of Birdland.

I'll sing louder, better and longer.

And I'll drown them all out.

# 7

—෴—

# Sweet Harmony

I decided not to say anything to Balwin about his father visiting me. Of course, Balwin was confused as to why his father was so cooperative about my coming over to practice music, giving him the car to pick me up, never questioning what we were doing and never complaining about the noise. It filled him with suspicions, and he often wondered aloud about it when I was there. I thought it would just break his heart even to think that I might be seeing him only because his father was paying me.

"It's almost as if he's happy I got into a fight at school," Balwin said. "My mother was far more upset than he was about it. In fact, she was the one to suggest I should stop seeing you."

"Maybe you should," I quickly said.

"No, no, it's all become nothing," he promised.

He was back in school and back at the piano for our chorus rehearsals. An unexpected and happy result of the fight and of all the trouble we both had with other students was Balwin's loss of shyness. He was no longer reluctant about talking to me and sitting with me at lunch. It was as if the fight had been some sort of initiation he had to endure in order to be accepted. Almost immediately afterward, fewer and fewer boys teased him, and those who did, didn't do it with any enthusiasm.

"They're making things up about us behind our backs anyway," Balwin rationalized after I had made a remark about it. He gazed around the cafeteria, still searching for wry smiles and sly glances.

"We never needed their permission to talk to each other, Balwin," I told him.

"Right. Who even cares about them?" he asked with his new bravado.

Despite my fury toward his father and the insulting proposal he had made to me, I had to admit to myself that what he had predicted was coming true anyway. Balwin began to take better care of himself. He loosened up, wore less formal clothing, actually had his hair styled and began to do more vigorous exercise and lose weight. I started to wonder if Balwin didn't suspect something because he began to report his losses to me on a regular basis, almost as if he believed I had some sort of personal stake in his physical improvement. After two and a half weeks, he was down ten pounds and it became very apparent in his face. His cheeks lost their plumpness and I thought he looked a lot more handsome.

Exercise made him proud of his budding muscularity. One afternoon, he just had to roll up his sleeves to show me his emerging biceps.

"My father's happy because I'm finally making use of the expensive weight lifting equipment he bought me three years ago."

I felt funny encouraging him. I couldn't help experiencing the guilt, even though I had specifically and vehemently turned down his father's offer. Nevertheless, Balwin was so excited and proud about his progress, I had to compliment him.

He no longer avoided physical education classes and he began to make friends with boys who previously had no use for him. Now they were inviting him to participate in their pickup basketball games and then, nearly a month after the fight he had had with Joey Adamson, I saw the two of them talking and joking with each other between classes as if they had been lifelong friends.

Even Thelma Williams began to eat her own words because some of her girlfriends were making positive remarks about Balwin's new look. Reluctantly, she approached me after our physical education class and said, "Looks like you're having a good influence on your man."

She spoke the words as though they each left the taste of rotten eggs in her mouth.

"Whatever he does, he does because he wants to do it. Not because of me," I said. "And he's not my man. He's his own man," I snapped.

Everyone's eyebrows went up. Even I was changing, talking more these days, and they all took note of it.

Thelma smirked, looked at the others and shook her head.

"Sure," she said. "Just shut him off and you'll see whose man he is and whose he isn't."

They all laughed and walked on, leaving me pondering what they all believed. Balwin and I had hardly exchanged a friendly kiss. What made them assume otherwise? Was it simply our spending so much time with each other?

"It's the music," I told Arlene Martin and Betty Lipkowski one afternoon when they asked me why I spent so much time with Balwin as compared to some of the better-looking, more-outgoing boys who had shown interest in me.

"Music?" Arlene asked.

"Balwin feels it like I do. When we're doing a song together, we're connected. We touch each other more deeply. In here," I said with my hand over my breast, "and here," I added pointing to my temple.

They sat there staring at me for a moment. Then Betty shook her head and smiled.

"You make it sound like sex," she said with an air of jealousy.

"Maybe it's better than sex," I said.

The two looked at each other and then gazed at me as if I was truly insane. Soon, there was something else about me and Balwin, something else to fill the pot of gossip and to be stirred and spread. Betty and Arlene were telling people we were in some kind of weird, kinky relationship related to music. It kept us on the idle-chatter theater marquee, kept us moving through spotlights and made us aware of every word we said to each other, every touch or smile. It was as if we both felt we were under glass, in the camera's eye, being recorded. Ironically, it made Balwin even more self-conscious about his appearance and he looked more handsome.

When I sang in chorus now, I could feel everyone's eyes and ears on me, watching how I gazed at Balwin behind the piano, all of them looking for some special light, some special sign that would reveal the magic we shared. I suppose I sang even better. I know I sang louder, but Mr. Glenn was very pleased.

"This will be the best concert ever," he predicted.

Two nights before the concert, Balwin picked me up for another special rehearsal at his house. He had completed his song about me and wanted me to hear all of that as well as complete our preparations for my second audition number. His father, pleased with

Balwin's physical changes, was talking about buying him his own car.

"He told me if I was going to have girlfriends and dates and such, there would be a greater need for my own transportation. I didn't even bring it up!" he cried, ecstatic over his father's new face.

Whenever his father greeted me now, he always wore a very pleased smile. Balwin said it was having an effect on their whole family. When his father was happy, his mother was happy.

"I can't believe the changes that have come over my home these past few weeks," he told me as we drove to his house. "My father and I actually talk to each other these days. I don't know how to explain it, but I'm sure it has a lot to do with you," he added.

"Me? Why?" I asked quickly.

He shrugged.

"I said I don't know how to explain it. All I know, Ice, is ever since you and I started working together, the world turned into rainbow colors from the gray and black it used to be. You're just going to have to accept the compliment," he insisted.

I turned from him, feeling my heart skip beats. These were nice things to hear said about me, but somehow they made me very anxious. It was as if my heart knew more than my brain and with every beat was warning me that rainbows don't come until after the storm.

We had yet to have the real storm.

* * *

Balwin's house was always very quiet, but this evening it seemed more so. His father didn't make his usual appearance in the living room doorway either.

"My parents are having dinner at the home of one of my father's clients," Balwin explained. "My mother wanted me to go, too, but I told her I had already made plans. My father said it was fine," Balwin quickly added before I could complain that he shouldn't have turned her down. He smiled at me and shook his head. "He is the one who always insists I go along to show my respect for his clients. I sure can't figure him out these days," he said and continued down the basement stairs.

A dark shadow moved over the hallway toward me, but it was only a cloud floating across the moon, shutting down the light that passed through the windows. I followed Balwin who was already at the piano.

"It's ready," he declared. "I've finally figured out the last verse."

I knew he was speaking about the song he had written for me.

I stood at the side of the piano and he began, singing through the part I had heard before and then looking at me during the finished final verse, he sang:

*Yes, there is music in the silence of her smile.*
*There is a melody in her eyes.*
*When she looks at me,*

*I feel my heart begin to sing.*
*I feel the glory that her lips can bring.*
*I understand the true reason for the spring*
*The burst of blossoms, the song of birds*
 *And I lift my own lips and eyes to be caressed*
  *by her bejeweled voice.*
*So play, play this song of you.*
*Play for the old and play it for the new.*
*Play at the break of day and play in the*
  *twilight hour.*
*Play away the sadness and the sorrow.*
*Walk before the saddest eyes you see.*
*Walk and bring the music back to me.*

When he lifted his fingers from the keys and sat back, I just stared at him. The music was still ringing in my ears. He formed a tentative, insecure smile.

"Is it all right?" he finally asked.

I nodded and then he stood up quickly, his face twisted with confusion.

"Ice," he said, "Ice, there are tears streaking down your cheeks. What is it?" he asked stepping closer. He touched one of my tears as if he had to feel it to believe it. Then he brought his fingers to his lips.

"Beautiful," I whispered.

"Like you," he said.

His face moved toward mine in such small incremental movements, it was truly slow motion, but I didn't step back or turn away. We kissed, a soft, long kiss, neither of us lifting our hands from our sides. When he pulled away, his eyes were still closed as if he was trying to savor every lingering delicious moment.

"When I kiss you, it's like bringing the words to the music, making it complete," he said.

I smiled and he kissed me again. His left hand went to my waist and his right to my shoulder. I put my arms around him and we held each other, our lips holding us as though all the magnetic magic was there at our mouths.

"The song was the only way I could tell you how I felt about you," he said softly. "I feel it all here," he added, placing his hand over his heart.

I nodded and he took me by the hand and walked me to the settee. We sat beside each other just looking at each other. When someone has so much creativity and talent inside him as Balwin has, I thought, it becomes a more solid identity, far deeper than any mask of male good looks. His feelings for me weren't only in his eyes and on his lips; they were in his very being. I was overwhelmed by his sincerity and his hunger for my approval and love.

Yet, I couldn't help feeling a little afraid as well, but not afraid for myself as much as I was afraid for him. Such total love as Balwin was expressing for me made someone, especially someone like him, as vulnerable as a turtle out of its shell. I did not know myself if I loved or cared for him half as much as he apparently cared for me. He longed to hear me say so. His eyes told me that.

But I did not know if what I felt for him at the moment was all or as much as any woman could feel for any man. Was this what love was? Instinctively, I felt that love meant caring for someone more than you cared for anyone else, even yourself, but I also understood that you needed him to feel the same way or you were incomplete, lost. Could I feel anywhere as intense about Balwin as he obviously could feel about me? Wouldn't he feel incomplete, lost, if I didn't? It took the greatest trust to utter the words, "I love you," to anyone because he might laugh or reject you and leave you as exposed as that turtle.

What would happen then?

Would you be afraid to ever utter those words again?

Silence, I realized, was so safe.

As if he could hear the debate in my mind, Balwin leaned forward to end it with a long and far more passionate kiss. He moved his lips over my cheek and up to my eyes. He kissed my forehead, my hair and then my lips again. I did not stop him or pull back and his excitement built faster and faster. I thought I could hear his heart beating against mine, or was that only my own, pounding?

"Ice," he whispered, his hands slipping under my blue cotton blouse and then up to my breasts. His fingers moved in quick side motions over my nipples, hardening them. My back softened and I lowered myself as he moved over me. I felt my bra clip snap and then his fingers on my skin, making every place he touched feel like a tiny firecracker had been lit over it, exploding, the heat building up and down my stomach and my chest, circling my ribs and making me soften and soften until I felt so helpless, so willing to be touched everywhere, kissed everywhere.

I closed my eyes and felt as if I was sinking into the settee.

"I love you, Ice. There, I said it without singing it," he bragged.

I opened my eyes and looked into his to see the great happiness. He kissed me again, his tongue slipping over mine and then he struggled with his own clothes until I felt his naked thighs and his hardened excitement emerging. It had the opposite effect from what I imagined it was supposed to have. It was more like a wake-up call, a quick splash of cold water or even an electric shock.

What was I doing?

Was this what I wanted to happen? And even so, was it what I wanted to happen now?

Had I already passed that moment when you could still think and decide, that moment before the heat in your blood took control and turned you into an obedient slave to your own passions?

"Wait, stop," I said. "Please, Balwin. Don't," I cried sharply.

He lifted himself from me and looked down, his eyes so hot, I could see the fire burning inside him. I shook my head.

"Oh," he moaned and then looked down at himself as if he just realized what he had been doing. "Oh. I'm sorry," he muttered and struggled to get himself dressed.

I sat up and fixed my bra. He rushed about, getting his clothes on, hurrying like someone who had to flee the scene of some crime. I reached out to touch his shoulder and he stopped and looked at me, his face full of desperation.

"I'm just not ready for that," I said.

He looked like he would burst into tears. He nodded quickly and completed dressing. Then he rose and for a moment looked in every direction.

"Well...we...well...let's get back to work," he said.

I watched him hurry back to the piano and sift through pages of music, keeping his eyes off me.

"I'm sorry. I know that wasn't fair of me," I said.

He looked up and started to shake his head.

"No, it wasn't fair of me. I wasn't sure myself," I admitted. I thought about a spiritual I often sang. "You weren't the only one in muddy waters," I told him.

He smiled.

"You mean you never..."

I shook my head.

He looked relieved.

"I'm no expert," I said, "but it seems to me it's

better if it takes its proper time. If it's meant to be, that is," I added.

"Like a baby being born?" he suggested. "You shouldn't rush it, huh?"

I laughed.

"Maybe. I'm no expert when it comes to that either," I said and he laughed too.

"Back to the music," he said and I rose to join him at the piano.

It was truly as if we had rid ourselves of some cobwebs, some of the darkness and the shadows that always hung between us like Spanish moss, draped over our every expression, our every word. We had to get past the feelings, the need to touch and know each other in more intimate ways before we could draw closer to each other than we already were. Once we had done that, the music followed, blossomed. His fingers were freed and so was my voice. We sounded so good together, we both cried out for joy, both knowing it was special.

"If you sing like that, you'll get in that school for sure," Balwin declared when we finished.

"I will if you come along to accompany me. Can you?"

"We've got to find out if they permit it first," he said. "If they do, sure I will."

"Thank you, Balwin. You've given me so much," I said.

I hugged him and he held on to me a moment

longer, his head pressed to my bosom, his eyes closed.

"You've given me much more," he whispered, his voice cracking.

I lifted his head away, looked down at his loving face and lowered myself to kiss him. The music, his devotion, made him the most handsome man in the world to me at that moment. His hands reached around my waist and pressed my rear as he brought his lips to my lower stomach and then lower and lower until I felt a rush of excitement shoot with lightning speed through my blood to my heart. He looked up at me again, his eyes drawing me. Did I have the strength to say, "stop," again?

Moving together, touching each other, even through mere looks and words, was like trying to navigate a minefield in which passion could explode at any time if we accidentally triggered it through a deeper look or an innocent caress.

"Step back, Ice," I told myself. "Hurry before it's nearly too late again."

However, my own fingers, like little traitors, betrayed me. They came around to undo my pants. Balwin began to lower them over my hips. His lips moved over my naked stomach, pushing into the waistband of my panties. I moaned as his hands went under them to grip my buttocks and hold me.

He breathed deeply as if he wanted to commit every aspect of me to his memory. Then, he lowered his arms, surrounding my legs behind the knees, and stood, lifting me.

"See how strong I've become?" he asked, smiling. I kissed him again and we were back on the settee. This time, I lay there quietly as he carefully and patiently removed every piece of clothing from my body, including my socks. Then he knelt at the settee and put his forehead on my stomach. My blood felt like it was at a boil. When he lifted his head and perused my body, I looked at him and saw the pleasure and the utter amazement and joy building in his eyes. He hovered over me, taunting me with his lips and his fingers.

"Turn off the lights," I whispered.

He rose to do so.

"I understand," he said. "You're not ready to see me like this yet. Got a ways to go, huh?"

"That's not it at all, Balwin."

"Sure it is. That's fine," he said. "I'll be there soon," he vowed.

He slipped out of his clothing and then lay beside me. We kissed and held each other.

"Muddy waters clearing any?" he asked.

I was so deep down in the well of passion, his voice seemed to reverberate above me. I was losing the battle. In fact, it might be all over, I thought. My own curiosity and excitement were pushing caution away from the controls. Alarms were being drowned out by the drumroll in my heart, the parade of desire and lust marching up from my thighs to the back of my neck and around to my lips.

He moved closer, closer...

And then, we heard the upstairs door open and close and his parents' voices, his father's laugh and his mother's following.

Balwin practically flew away from me, scurrying like a rodent over the floor to gather his clothes. I rushed to get mine on as well.

"The lights!" I cried. "They'll wonder why we're down here in the dark."

He flicked on the lamp at the piano just as we heard the door to the basement being opened. I rushed around the corner to keep out of eyesight as I completed dressing. Balwin tapped out some notes, pretending to be working at the piano.

"Hey!" his father called down. "You still working with Ice down there?"

"Yes, Dad."

"Getting late, son," he said and closed the door.

I came around quickly and we looked at each other. Most of the lights had been off. Surely, it looked suspicious and strange.

"It's all right," Balwin said trying to reassure me. "Don't worry."

"I'd better get home," I said. He nodded and we started up the stairs.

When we stepped into the hallway, his father appeared in the living room doorway, gazing at us, a wry smile on his face.

"Making music down there?" he asked.

Balwin looked at me, his eye shifting every which way as he searched desperately for just the right answer.

"Yes," I said for him.

"Good," his father said. He smiled at me. "Good," he continued and turned away.

We hurried out and to the car.

"Sorry about all that," Balwin said as we drove off.

"Maybe we had better cool it for a while," I suggested.

"Just awhile," he said nodding. "We'll start again after the concert Saturday, okay?"

"We'll see," I said.

Little did I know what my hesitation would come to mean to him, but then, I had no idea myself.


Our annual spring concert was always a very well-attended affair. We had an excellent, award-winning orchestra as well as an award-winning chorus. Many people attended who didn't even have students participating. They just knew they would get their money's worth buying a ticket to one of our concerts.

Most of the proceeds went toward a scholarship for a worthy musical student. The winner or winners were announced just before the final choral number of the evening. Mr. Glenn called up the principal to make the presentation. Everyone was sure that Balwin would be this year's recipient. After all, he had volunteered his services for the chorus for more than two years now and had even performed solo at past concerts, always bringing the audience to its feet.

Despite his father's reluctance to praise Balwin for his musical abilities, the accolades and the congratulations he and Mrs. Noble received made it impossible for him not to at least appear proud. It wasn't hard to see, however, that he had hopes Balwin would eventually go on to pursue a career that held more financial promise. Balwin told me that if he hadn't been chosen in an early admissions program to attend Juilliard, his father would surely have pressured him to go to Harvard or Yale, both of which had accepted him, and then get an MBA.

"He's got to get it out of his system," was Mr. Noble's favorite expression whenever anyone talked to him about Balwin's pursuit of music. It was as if he believed music was like an infectious disease or something, a flu or virus he had to purge from his soul. Mr. Noble seemed to think that with time, Balwin would simply outgrow it.

All this applause was nice, he told friends, but when it came right down to it, applause didn't put food on the table or pay for an elegant home or provide a good living. For that, Balwin would eventually have to turn his attention to more mundane things like following in his footsteps perhaps and becoming a financial advisor, manager or even a company chief financial officer. He could always buy a piano and play for people on holidays, couldn't he?

"After all, how many people do you know," his father would ask someone, "who make a very good living on entertainment?

"We all can't be Frank Sinatra," he pointed out with a laugh.

I heard him say these very things in the auditorium lobby during the concert's intermission. Balwin heard them, too, and was embarrassed enough to try to lose himself in the crowd.

"I've got to check on something," he told his mother and slipped away.

My mama and daddy had come to the concert. I was surprised Mama had actually shown up, even though she had gone into her room to prepare long before I left. She always thought the music was too stuffy and made her sleepy. I had to admit that she looked very nice, dressed in a dark blue dress with her pearls and her hair and makeup perfect. She was enjoying a lot of attention, and every once in a while, glanced at me with her eyes dancing, brightly filled with pride. Daddy looked somewhat uncomfortable beside her, his tie like a hangman's noose on his neck. He flashed me a smile and made his eyes roll toward Mama who had just let out one of her sweet sounding laughs while she absorbed a compliment from someone else's father.

We were called back in to finish the concert. The second half began with three orchestra numbers and then a chorus number, after which the auditorium grew very quiet. Mr. Glenn introduced the principal who stepped forward and announced that this year the school had extremely worthy recipients for its prestigious music scholarships. He then began with a very detailed rendition of all of Balwin's accomplishments. I had forgotten myself how he had often gone over to the elementary school to help that chorus rehearse and once had performed a small assembly program for the primary classes.

The audience rose to its feet when he was called forward to receive his scholarship. I clapped as hard as I could. He glanced my way and smiled and then stepped up and thanked the school and his parents. He promised to make good use of the scholarship.

Again, there was a hush in the crowd. The principal put on his reading glasses and began by describing someone who was truly a discovery, "a jewel so covered in modesty, someone could walk right by her. Until," he added lifting his head to look out at the audience, "you heard her sing. Then, there is no question. It is with great joy that we present a scholarship to someone who has the potential to make us very proud citizens of this school, Ice Goodman."

At first, I didn't realize he had uttered my name. I stood there, waiting for another name. Mr. Glenn turned to me, beaming, and the others looked at me, too. All their eyes brought the reality home. I thought I would be unable to take a single step, but Mr. Glenn came forward and reached for my hand to escort me to the podium. Balwin's face was so full of joy, his eyes glittered like tiny stars in the footlights. I thought I would surely faint. My heart was beating so fast, I couldn't find a breath.

The principal handed me the envelope and stepped back. I knew that meant I had to say something. Everyone in the auditorium was looking at me, waiting.

"Thank you," I said. Then I turned and hurried back to my place.

No one applauded.

The principal stepped forward, laughing.

"She makes up for all that when she opens her mouth to sing, folks. Just sit back and enjoy the final number."

The audience finally applauded.

I did sing hard and strong until the final note, after which Mr. Glenn congratulated me first and then most of the chorus. Balwin and I remained backstage waiting to greet our parents. Mama was in her glory. She feasted on the accolades and compliments as if she had expected them, and then Daddy revealed that they had been informed of my impending award so that they would be sure to attend the concert.

"We're very proud of you, honey, very proud," he said hugging me.

Some of the men he knew pulled him off to shake

hands and receive their congratulations. Balwin and I stood close to each other, greeting people like the victors of some Olympic event. Finally, his father came up to me.

"I guess your working together helped you both in different ways," he began. Balwin was shaking hands, but listening with one ear turned our way.

I nodded, smiled and started to turn away from his father, when he reached out again and took my hand.

"You deserve this," he said. "And now that I know you've got a promising future, it will be put to good use, I'm sure. Thanks for fulfilling the bargain," he said.

I opened my hand and looked down at five crisp hundred-dollar bills.

Balwin gazed at it as well and then he looked up at me, his face full of confusion and pain.

"No," I said shaking my head. "I don't want your money, Mr. Noble," I cried. "I told you..."

He turned his back on me and walked into the crowd. I looked at Balwin.

"I told him I didn't want..."

He didn't wait for me to finish. He moved away quickly, disappearing into the crowd. I started after him, but Mama seized me and started to praise me in front of her friends, claiming how much she encouraged me to sing in church. Half of me listened.

The other half was off, screaming into the night.

# 8

—∿—

# Wounded

The silence I had once embraced as a friend soon turned into a despised enemy. It was the silence I heard growing between Balwin and me almost the instant the incident with the money occurred in front of him. The pain he felt was so deep, I thought I could never reach down far enough to wipe the salve of my explanations over it. He would always suspect, distrust, even detest me as long as he had any reason to believe I had been part of a conspiracy hatched by his father.

Full of a thousand anxieties, I tried calling him as soon as I was home from the concert, but he didn't answer his phone and when his father picked up their main phone, he told me Balwin was already asleep.

"You did a despicable thing handing me that money in front of him, Mr. Noble. He thinks everything between us was planned, contrived, done for the money," I said, tears burning under my eyelids.

"Wasn't it?" his father asked coldly.

A hot rush of blood heated my face.

"No!" I screamed, "and I want you to take your money back."

He laughed.

"Sure you do," he said. "Mail it to me," he challenged and hung up.

I found an envelope immediately and addressed it. Then I stuffed the money in it and set it out to mail it to him first thing in the morning. Balwin's mother answered his phone the next day and told me he had gone for a ride with some friends. I didn't know whether to believe her or not. I asked her to tell Balwin I had called and she said she would, but I didn't hear from him, and I decided not to keep calling.

Of course, we saw each other in school the following Monday, but as soon as he set eyes on me, he turned and headed in the opposite direction. His avoidance of me caused more of a stir than when we had begun to be together. Everyone wanted to know what was going on, but I ignored the questions and the comments, all except one: Thelma Williams's implication that Balwin was upset he had to share the award with me.

"The only reason why you don't know how stupid that is," I told her, "is because you're so stupid."

It nearly started a bad fight. If Balwin heard about it, he didn't say anything to me before the day ended.

Chorus was over for the year so we didn't meet after school, but on my way home, I saw him driving his car in my direction. When I rounded the corner to my street, I found him parked alongside the curb. He was staring ahead, waiting.

I got in and closed the door.

"I heard about you and Thelma Williams," he began. "Thanks for defending me."

"It was a dumb thing for her to say."

He nodded and then he squinted at me.

"I just want to know if everything you did was paid for with that money my father gave you," he said.

"Nothing was paid for, Balwin. I've been trying to tell you that, but you won't listen."

He stared at me, the pain and hurt tearing at his eyes.

"Why didn't you tell me what my father had done? Why didn't you ever say anything about it?"

"I thought you would always be suspicious. I thought you would never believe it wasn't true," I replied. "I also thought your father would get so angry, he would forbid you from ever seeing me."

"You should have told me," he repeated, shaking his head. "If you like someone, really like him, you trust him. Trust is a very important thing, Ice, very important."

"I know. I'm sorry, Balwin. Really, I am. I sent the money back to him. When I called and told him, he said I wouldn't and he laughed at the idea."

"You called?"

"A few times. I called your phone and spoke to your mother, too. Didn't anyone give you the messages?"

He shook his head.

"I guess they thought my usefulness was ended," I said. I was feeling so sorry for myself, I wished someone would dig me a well to cry in. "Your father didn't have to pay me to like you and to help you feel better about yourself, Balwin."

I turned on him, my eyes burning with unrequited tears.

"I enjoyed every minute we were together and the song you wrote for me will always be something special to me."

Balwin glanced at me and I stared at the floor. I was afraid to look directly at him again, afraid I really might start to cry and never stop. I think he sensed it. His voice turned so much softer.

"I should have given you more of a chance to explain, Ice. I'm sorry about that, but I was so hurt, so angry. I felt betrayed."

"I know."

"Will you come back?"

"No," I said. "I don't think I'll feel comfortable there just now."

"Well, then let's keep practicing at school. Mr. Glenn will let us use the chorus room, okay?"

I was silent.

"Ice? Okay?"

"If that's what you really want," I said.

"I do."

"Then, okay," I said and got out of the car.

"Tomorrow, after school?" he called.

I nodded.

Then I turned and walked away. He watched me walk all the way to my apartment building before he started his car and left. I watched him drive off.

Music, I thought, music was still the tie that binds. The rhythm, the melody and the words flowed through my heart as well as my mind. I could face anything if that was always true, I thought.

I was soon to be put to the test.

It came in the form of a loud knock on our apartment door just a little after eleven that same evening. Mama was already asleep and when she fell asleep, she was pretty much dead to the world. Sometimes, she even put cotton in her ears to keep anything from disturbing her.

I thought the knocking was part of a dream I was having. I tossed and turned all night, fretted in and out of the nightmare trying to settle in my brain. I heard the knocking continue and finally opened my eyes. I listened, heard a voice and more knocking and then rose quickly, scooping up my robe and shoving my feet into my slippers.

"Who's there?" I called through the closed door. There were two robberies this month in the building, and both had happened because someone had opened her door too quickly.

"Mike Tooey, from the agency," I heard. I knew that was Daddy's security company and I knew Mike Tooey. I looked toward Mama's bedroom, but she hadn't yet woken.

"Just a minute," I said and undid the locks. I opened the door and faced him. He had his hat in his hands and he was in full uniform. "What is it?"

"Your dad," he said, "was shot about an hour ago. He was stopping a robbery."

I pressed my hand to my breast. My whole body felt as if I had fallen into a large pot of boiling water. I could barely move a muscle.

"How is he?" I finally managed to ask.

"He's in intensive care at the hospital. You and your mother should get over there," he said. "Sorry."

Sorry? It sounded so simple, so nonchalant, so nothing. Sorry to wake you. Sorry I stepped on your foot. Sorry I snapped at you. Sorry I bumped into you. Sorry your father was shot.

"I can take you two there," he offered. "I'll wait outside in the company car, okay?"

I nodded, closed the door, took a deep breath and started for Mama's bedroom.

There was no music in my mind, just the continuous, ominous roll of parade drums.

Almost as if she knew she would be facing unhappiness when she woke, Mama stubbornly clung to sleep as I shook her. I shook her again and called her and shook her until finally her eyelids fluttered, closed, and then snapped open.

"What?" she practically screamed at me.

"Daddy's been shot," I said.

She stared up at me a moment and then she sat up so quickly and firmly, I stepped back.

"What?"

"Mike Tooey is outside waiting to take us to the hospital in the company car," I said. "Daddy stopped a robbery."

"Oh Jesus," she muttered, "oh Jesus, Jesus."

She rose and began to get dressed. I hurried back to my room to do the same. Less than ten minutes later, I was ready, but Mama was still brushing her hair.

"I look a mess," she moaned at her own image in the mirror.

"I don't think that matters at the moment, Mama," I said dryly.

She paused and looked at me as if I had gone crazy.

"It always matters, child. You think I want your father looking at a hag when I get there. The better I look, the better he's going to feel," she predicted, finished her hair and then joined me at the door. "I shoulda bought that wig the other day," she muttered as we hurried out. "You got a wig, you just throw it on and don't worry. I should have bought it."

Mr. Tooey either really didn't know very much or was too frightened to give us the details. However, we were told everything almost as soon as we arrived at the ER. Daddy had taken two bullets; the first had lodged in his shoulder, but the second had hit him in the abdomen and nicked his spine as it passed through. He had lost a lot of blood and was in critical condition.

"Is he going to live?" Mama demanded from the doctor.

"We'll see," was the doctor's best reply no matter how much Mama pressured him.

Different places have different kinds of silences, I thought as we waited in the lounge anxiously. Hospitals weren't really quiet places. Staff workers, interns, nurses, all spoke rather loudly to each other. There was much activity going on, too: people being pushed along in wheelchairs or on stretchers, doctors talking to relatives or to the patients themselves, technicians rolling machines from one room to another, nurses and doctors shouting orders across hallways.

The silences I did see and hear were the silences in the eyes of the worried wives, mothers, husbands, brothers, sisters and friends who lingered in corridors, quietly comforting each other, holding each other, standing in the shadows and gazing absently at the floors or walls or looking out the windows at nothing, just waiting in a world where all time seemed to have stopped, where everything said or done seemed so far off reverberating into the darkness.

There were many elective mutes here, many people who didn't want to speak, to hear the sounds of their own voices for fear it would make them crumble or turn to tears and cries of pain.

"Will my daddy die?"

"Will Bobby get better?"

"When will the doctor tell us anything?"

"When will my mommy come home?"

It was so much better not to hear these and similar questions, not to have to answer, not to have to look into the face of reality and recognize what tomorrow could be like. It was better to wait quietly, to hold your breath and not think about anything, anything at all.

Mama couldn't do that. She talked incessantly, commenting to everyone who would listen, complaining about the waiting, the world today, the criminals out there, her poor husband's miserable fate, moaning and groaning, drawing all the sympathy she could to herself until finally, exhausted, she sputtered like some boat running out of fuel on some lake, her words growing farther and farther apart, half spoken, and soon altogether stopped.

She stared along with the others and waited and looked at me and took a deep breath and closed her eyes.

Time tormented us. Minutes took longer. Hours stretched. We were stuck in forever, until eventually, almost like an afterthought brought back from some dark corner of the hospital, the doctor made his way toward us, his face glum, a doctor's face full of ifs and maybes.

Daddy was still alive. The next twenty-four to forty-eight hours were critical. If he lived, it would be a long recuperation with a lot of therapy. He would most likely regain his ability to walk, too, but it was all somewhere way out there like a promise at the end of a rainbow.

It was best we went home and returned the next day. There wasn't much left to do, but wait.

"He's a strong man, Mrs. Goodman," the doctor told her. "A lesser man would be gone by now," he said. I could see he meant it sincerely.

Mama nodded. For once, she seemed speechless. She threaded her arm through mine and we left to get a cab to take us home. All the way she rested her head against my shoulder. As soon as we arrived, she went right to sleep.

I sat in the living room for a while, looking at Daddy's empty chair and humming some music to myself. Finally, I went to bed and fell asleep, too exhausted to entertain a single dream.

I was up and out of bed the moment my eyes snapped open in the morning. Mama was still asleep. I went right to the phone and called the hospital. When they heard I was immediate family, they forwarded my call to the nurse on duty who told me Daddy was stable, but there was nothing more to say until the doctor came to evaluate.

I rushed about the apartment, putting up some coffee first because I knew Mama wouldn't budge without some. Then I called to her and woke her. She mumbled and cursed and cried, but finally rose. I showered and dressed and had her coffee poured and waiting when she emerged from her room, practically sleepwalking to the table. I told her I had called the hospital and what the nurse had said.

"We've got to get there as quicky as we can, Mama. We've got to talk to the doctor."

"Why rush? All they do is make you wait and wait until they're good and ready," she said.

"We don't want to miss him," I insisted. "If you're not ready, I'll leave without you," I threatened.

She looked up at me with surprise and then shook her head and complained all the rest of the time and all the way to the hospital, moaned about how I had hurried her so much she couldn't fix herself properly to face the world. I was to be blamed for her mediocre appearance. I worked hard at closing her out of my mind and soon her words bounced off my ears like raindrops off the top of an umbrella.

I was right about being there as soon as we could. The doctor was on his way to another hospital after seeing Daddy and we wouldn't have gotten any direct information if we hadn't been there.

"He's improved far faster and better than I had anticipated," he told us. "I believe he's out of danger, but he's going to begin a long recuperation. Prepare yourselves for that," he warned, his eyes on Mama as if he could sense how difficult it was going to be for her, maybe even more difficult than it would be for Daddy.

He told us we could see Daddy later in the day when he was conscious. I had the hardest time keeping Mama at the hospital to wait for the opportunity. She wanted to go home and dress herself all over again. We ate some lunch in the hospital cafeteria and then went back to the ICU waiting room and waited for the nurse to come out to get us.

"You can stay ten minutes," she said. "He's conscious now."

"Well, Hallelujah!" Mama muttered.

We followed the nurse in to Daddy's bedside. Even on his back with all the tubes and monitoring devices attached to him, he still looked big and powerful to me.

He smiled when he saw us.

"Now look what you've gone and done," Mama told him immediately. "I bet you didn't have to stick your big neck out, Cameron Goodman. I bet you just couldn't wait to be a hero, huh?"

"Hi Daddy," I said. I kissed him.

Mama looked around, held her face of chastisement, but kissed him, too.

"Now, what are we supposed to do?" she asked him.

"Mama," I whispered. "Don't cause him any worry now."

"You'll be fine," Daddy said. "Money comes in anyway. Insurance. Don't worry," he said.

"Great," Mama said. "And you have a long recuperation. You'll be hanging around the house playing that music all day and night now. I'm telling you right now, Cameron, I'm no good as a nurse," she warned.

Daddy smiled at me.

"Well, I'm not. I won't be carrying bedpans and breaking my nails changing bandages and such."

"There's home nursing care when we need it," Daddy told her, his voice just above a whisper. "Stop your worrying, Lena. You'll be fine. We'll all be fine."

"Right. Getting in the way of a bullet. I do declare, Cameron, I never wanted you to do this job. You shoulda…shoulda drove a taxi or something."

Daddy widened his smile, but I could see he was fading again fast.

"Don't worry," he whispered and fell asleep.

"You'll have to leave," the nurse said quickly.

"Leave? We haven't been here five minutes!" Mama cried.

"Please," the nurse insisted.

I took Mama's arm and practically walked her out forcibly. She muttered to herself until we were in the hall.

"You see his face when he looked up at me? I knew I wasn't looking my best," she cried. "We rushed here for five minutes. I'm going home," she said. "I'll be back tomorrow or when I can see him for a sensible visit. I'm so tired from all this, Ice. It's as if the bullets hit me, too."

Mama was more comfortable feeling sorry for herself and getting me to sympathize. I took her home, checked on Daddy with a phone call later and then made dinner for Mama and myself. She wanted me to return to school the next day, but I wouldn't do it. I went to the hospital and saw Daddy without her in the morning. He had improved some more and was stronger and more alert.

"Don't let this stop you from following your plans, Ice. Please," he begged me. "I was so proud of you at the concert."

"I don't know, Daddy. We've got so much more to think about now."

"There's nothing more. I'll be fine and so will your mama," he insisted. "Promise me," he insisted. "Promise."

"Okay, Daddy," I said. "I promise."

"Good." He closed his eyes with some relief. "Good," he said and fell asleep.

The news about Daddy spread fast through the school. When I returned the next day, everyone, especially my teachers, asked about him. Balwin was very attentive, feeling even worse about the misunderstanding that had occurred between us.

"You're still going to work on the audition, aren't you?" he asked.

"I don't know," I said. "Our lives are changed now. Daddy's going to require a long period of recuperation and I'm not sure about costs and money. I don't know," I told him.

He looked sicker about it than I was.

"Well, you should practice and keep up anyway," he said. "Just in case it works out."

"I don't know where I'll find the time," I said.

Now, as soon as school ended every day, I rushed over to the hospital to be with Daddy. Mama didn't visit as much and hated being in a hospital. I started to complain about it, but Daddy stopped me and said he was better off being around her only when she was happy. I understood and ignored her selfishness as best I could.

When Daddy was moved to a room, I found I could be a real help, assisting the nurse's aides, getting him things he needed or wanted or just amusing him. Every once in a while, he would look at me and make me repeat my promise to go forward with my plans. Finally, one day it dawned on him that I was spending so much time in the hospital, I couldn't be practicing my music.

"You've got your homework and end of the year exams, I know," he said. "Why are you spending so much time here, Ice? That boy still wants to help you, right?"

"Daddy—"

"You promised me, child. You telling me you're not keeping up the promise? You're my hope, Ice. I don't want to get out of this bed if you don't try. Well?"

"All right, Daddy," I said. "All right. I'll go back to practicing."

That satisfied him. It was left as an understanding between us, however, that I wouldn't discuss it with Mama. We both knew it would just create more tension in an already tense household.

She made her appearances when she thought she looked pretty enough. She paraded in as if she had just come off a model's runway. We could smell her perfume ten minutes before she arrived. When Daddy told her so, she shook her head angrily and said, "Well, I've got to do something to keep these putrid hospital odors out of my nose, don't I? You walk out of here smelling like a nurse if you don't," she insisted.

Daddy and I looked at each other and laughed.

"Go on, make fun of me, if you like, but I know I'm right," she insisted.

When Daddy was well enough to begin some therapy, I decided to meet with Balwin and go over my music. I still had my audition date for the Senetsky school scheduled. He and I practiced after school. It was very difficult for me to start again. It was as if we had never worked on the songs before, but Balwin was patient and kept giving me encouragement.

"Sometimes I think this is more important to you than it is to me," I told him.

He laughed.

"You just don't know yet how important it is to

you," he assured me. "But you will. Someday, you will and then you'll be happy you did this, Ice."

I smiled at him and then, almost as if it was a reflex action, I gave him a kiss. His eyes brightened like candles just lit.

"Tomorrow," he said, "I'd like to visit your father with you. I'll take you there after school," he said.

I thought that was very nice of him and when we arrived, Daddy was very happy to see him. They talked about music as if they had been old friends. Daddy was impressed with Balwin's knowledge of jazz. At the end, he thanked him for helping me.

"Your father's a great guy," Balwin told me. "I found it easier talking with him than I do with my own father," he added.

I felt sorry for him. At least I had someone who wanted the same things for me that I wanted for myself, someone encouraging me, standing beside me. Balwin was far lonelier than I had imagined, even lonelier than I was.

The next day Mama found out that Balwin had accompanied me to the hospital. She cross-examined Daddy about it and when I returned home, she started on me.

"What have you been doing with that fat boy?" she demanded.

"He's not a fat boy anymore, Mama. He's still trimming down nicely and—"

"Oh, I don't care about none of that. What's going on, Ice?"

Reluctantly, I revealed that our practicing for the audition had continued and she went off on me like she never had before, screaming at the top of her voice, tossing things around the kitchen, straining her neck and her eyes to the point of bursting blood vessels.

"First, where we ever going to find the money for such nonsense, and second, how am I supposed to handle your father with you gone, huh? You can forget all that talk about going to some fancy school and stop wasting everyone's time, Ice. I'm going to need you right here."

I didn't argue with her, but that didn't stop her. She threatened to complain to Daddy about it. She even promised to tell him to stay in the hospital if I was going to leave for some school. Terrified of what damage she would do, I finally promised her I would stop practicing and cancel the audition. She was satisfied and calmed down, but slowly, muttering to herself almost until she fell asleep.

I told Balwin the next day. He tried to argue with me, but I wouldn't listen.

"We've only got one more week, Ice. Don't give up now," he pleaded.

I shook my head.

"It was silly of me to do this, Balwin, and wrong of me to waste your time too. I'm sorry. It's all so impossible, don't you see?"

"No," he said.

"Well it is," I told him and left.

I went home and put my music sheets away, took care of the chores in the house and made dinner, but Mama didn't come home for dinner. I ate alone. I thought she might have gone to the hospital and went as soon as I had cleaned up, but she wasn't there. I tried not telling Daddy about her, but he could read my face as if my thoughts were behind a glass wall.

"The woman's just frustrated," he said. "Don't fret about her. She'll be all right once I'm out of here," he promised. "How's your work going with Balwin? It's getting close to that time, right?"

I called on all my powers to hide the truth, but there was something so strong between Daddy and myself that he could feel the vibrations in my body. His eyes grew small with suspicion.

"Ice?"

"It's foolish to waste time on something like this, Daddy. Where are we going to get the money and you'll need me for a while. Maybe—"

"Ice," he nearly shouted. He was in a wheelchair and we were in the corner of the recreation room in the therapy area. Some people looked our way for a moment. Daddy reached out and seized my hand.

"You don't know what this has come to mean to me," he began. "I put all my dreams in you. All my disappointments are piled up and waiting to be crushed. You're the hope, honey. I watched you grow into this, take on the music like some magnificent, beautiful gown and go strutting across the stage. You've brought me the only joy I've had these years. And you're just starting. I know it, Ice. I know it in here," he said holding his hand over his heart. "Don't give up on me now.

"Don't be me," he declared firmly. "You go right home from here and you go into my third dresser drawer. You lift the clothes in the right corner and you take out that trumpet mouthpiece, understand?

"You hold it tightly in your hand and you think of me selling my trumpet and spending my whole life wondering 'what if?' And you take that mouthpiece with you to the audition. Do it for me and forget all the rest.

"Will you? Will you?"

"Yes, Daddy," I promised.

He reached out and touched the tear zigzagging down my cheek.

And he smiled.

"You're melting, Ice," he said laughing, "and it's just fine.

"Just fine."

# Epilogue

—⚬—

Balwin drove me. We had asked and been given permission for him to be my accompanist. Mama knew nothing about it. She thought I was going to school as usual and then going to visit Daddy.

I think my heart pounded all the way to New York City. When we arrived at the little theater, I was so terrified, I couldn't move my legs. I looked at Balwin and he laughed.

"I've seen stage fright and I've seen stage fright," he said, "but you've got stage terror."

"It's not funny, Balwin. I'm going to make a fool of myself," I cried.

"Then you'll make one of me, too," he declared firmly. He held out his hand and I got out of the car. "Take a deep breath," he said. "Close your eyes and take a deep breath. Go on. Relax yourself. This is nothing. If she doesn't like you, it's her loss, not yours."

"Right," I said. "Sure."

He laughed and we entered the theater. It was so quiet and empty, I thought we had come on the wrong day. Suddenly, a tall, thin dark-haired woman emerged from the shadows, her heels clicking on the tile floor of the small lobby.

"Are you this Ice Goodman?" she asked holding a paper in her right hand. She had large brown eyes and a sharp nose, so pointed at the tip, I thought she could cut steak with it.

"Yes," I said.

"You're ten minutes early, but that's fine. Madam Senetsky is in the theater. And this is your accompanist?" she asked nodding at Balwin.

"Balwin Noble," Balwin said extending his hand. She simply looked at it and nodded.

"Go right to the stage and begin," she ordered, turned and retreated into the theater.

"Ready?" Balwin asked.

"No," I said.

"Good," he said and led the way.

It was dark except for some small light on the stage. It took a moment for my eyes to get used to the auditorium. At first I thought there was no one there and then I saw someone sitting all the way in the rear.

Balwin continued down the aisle to the piano. He

sat, set out the music and looked at me. Then he nodded at the stage.

"Just do it as we have been," he said.

I looked back toward the woman in the rear. She
was like a manikin. I couldn't make out much detail,
but I saw that her hair was pulled tightly up into a
coiled chignon at the top of her head, a little toward
the rear where it was clipped. Why weren't there
more people here, I wondered, and where was that
tall, sour-looking woman who had greeted us?

Shaking, I stepped up onto the stage. Balwin had
me do a quick warm-up and then I looked at him and
he nodded. I took a deep breath and he began.

I sang as best I could. As I went on, I felt myself
relax and I thought only of the song itself and then, as
if by magic, I thought I saw Daddy sitting in the first
row, looking up and me and smiling.

And in his hand was his trumpet mouthpiece.

I did my second piece, too. No one spoke to us afterward. In fact, the elderly woman was gone when I
stepped off the stage. We stood for a while and then
realized no one was going to talk to us, so we started
out, looked in the lobby and found no one.

"Why couldn't someone at least thank us for coming or say good-bye?" I muttered.

Balwin shook his head.

"I guess they don't thank you. You thank them," he
said and we left.

He was very quiet most of the way home. I knew what he was thinking. It was a disaster. It was so bad we didn't even rate a good-bye and thanks for the effort. I felt sick to my stomach. The only thing that cheered me a bit was knowing Mama would be happy I failed. I wasn't going to tell her anything though. She would be so angry that I had gone to the audition in the first place.

I didn't forget about the audition, but all of the days right before graduation and the school year's end seemed full of small explosions and exhilaration. You could hear it in everyone's voices, how they burst with happiness and excitement. Lives were being planned. There was talk of colleges and jobs. It seemed as if a grand doorway was slowly opening for everyone to pass through into a new world, everyone but me.

Daddy made more progress with his therapy and there was talk now of his coming home. He and I didn't discuss the audition. It was left hanging in the air like some dream. I think he was afraid of my being disappointed and what that would do to him as well.

Mama carried on more about the new demands that would be made on her, but I could see she was happy about Daddy's impending return, too. With it was the promise of some sort of restoration. Daddy even added to her optimism by talking about their moving to a nicer place. He had compensation funds and he was promised a softer, easier job when he could return to work. He was, after all, something of a hero to the company.

When I had filled out my application, I had indicated I wanted Madam Senetsky to respond to Mr. Glenn at the school. I was afraid of anything arriving at the apartment and Mama finding it first. Finally, three days before the last day of school, the principal called me to his office. Mr. Glenn was there, too. The moment I walked in, I knew something astounding had occurred. Their faces radiated with congratulations.

I read the letter of acceptance signed by Madam Senetsky twice before really absorbing it. Once more in my life, I was muted, unable to speak. They laughed and congratulated me again. Mr. Glenn had Balwin called to the office. When he heard what had happened, he started to cry. It wasn't sobbing; it was just the emergence of some tears he quickly flicked away.

He and I left the building with the principal's permission and Balwin drove me to the hospital. Daddy was doing some upper body exercises in his wheelchair. The therapist turned when Daddy stopped and stared at us entering the therapy center.

I didn't speak.

I didn't have to speak.

What I did was hold up his trumpet mouthpiece.

He cried out and then, to the amazement of his therapist he stood up and took a few unassisted steps toward me. I ran into his arms.

"Mama will be furious," I said.

"So what's new about that?" he replied and we laughed.

"How can we do it, Daddy?"

"We can," he insisted, "and we will. I mean, you will."

Balwin nodded in agreement.

Outside the therapy room window, on the ledge, a sparrow paraded and flapped its wings.

And I remembered a little girl, afraid to speak, finding a voice in the music, the same music that helped the sparrow lift itself away to soar in the wind.

**POCKET BOOKS
PROUDLY PRESENTS**

# *ROSE*

# V.C. ANDREWS®

**Available September 2001
from
Pocket Books**

**Turn the page for a preview of
*ROSE*....**

I always believed there was something different about my father. He was whimsical and airy, light of foot and so smooth and graceful, he could slip in and out of a room full of people without anyone realizing he was gone. I don't think I ever saw him depressed or even deeply concerned about anything, no matter how dark the possibilities were. He lost jobs, had cars repossessed, saw his homes go into foreclosure. Twice that I knew of, he was forced to declare personal bankruptcy. There was even a time when we left one of our homes with little more than we carried on our very selves. Yet he never lost his spirit or betrayed his unhappiness in his voice.

I used to imagine him as a little boy stumbling and rolling over and over until he stopped and jumped right to his feet, smiling, with a big "Ta Da," as if his accident was an accomplishment. He was actually expecting applause, laughter, and encouragement after a fiasco. He once told me that when he received a failing grade on a test in school, he took joy in having a bright red mark on his paper while the other, less fortunate students who happened to have passed had only the common black. Defeat was never in his vocabulary. Every mistake, every failure was merely a minor setback and what was a setback anyway? Just an opportunity to start anew. Pity the poor successful ones who spent their whole lives in one town, in one job, in one house.

Daddy's impulsiveness and childlike joy in leaping out of one persona into another in an instant annoyed my mother to no end. She always seemed embarrassed by his antics and depressed by his failures, yet she held on to him like someone clinging to a wayward sailboat in a storm, hoping the wind would die down, the rain would stop, and soon, maybe just over the horizon, there would be sunny skies. On what she built these sails full of optimism, I never knew. Maybe that was her fantasy: believing in Daddy—a fantasy I thought belonged only to a young and innocent daughter, me.

At least we remained in one state, Georgia, crisscrossing and vaulting towns, cities, villages; however, it soon became obvious that Daddy anticipated his inevitable defeats. After a while—our second mortgage failure, I think—we stopped buying and started renting for as short a period as the landlords tolerated. Daddy loved six-month leases. He called every new rental a trial period, a romance. Who knew if it was what we wanted or if it would last, so why get too committed? Why get committed to anything?

Of course, Mommy flung the usual arguments at him.

"Rose needs a substantial foundation. She can't do well in school moving like this from place to place. She can't make friends and neither can I, Charles.

"And neither can you!" she emphasized, her eyebrows nearly leaping off her face. "You don't do anything with other men like most men do. You don't watch ball games or go out hunting and fishing with buddies and it's no wonder. You don't give yourself a chance to build a friendship, a relationship. Before you see someone for the second time, you're packing suitcases."

My father would listen as if he was really giving all that serious thought and then he would shake his head and say something like, "There's no such thing as friends anyway, just acquaintances, Monica."

"Good. Let me at least have a long enough life somewhere to have acquaintances," Mommy fired back at him.

He laughed and nodded.

"You will," he promised. "You will."

Daddy made promises like children blow bubbles. At
the first suggestion of approaching storm clouds, he blew
his promises at us: perfectly shaped, rainbow-colored
hopes and dreams, and stood back watching them float and
bob around us. When they popped, he just reached into his
bag of tricks and started a new bubble. I felt like we were
all swimming in a glass of champagne.

At present, he was a car salesman in Lewisville, Georgia, a small community about forty-five miles northwest of
Atlanta. Lewisville was famous for its duck ponds and its
one industry, Lewis Foundry, which manufactured auto-
motive cast-iron braking components and employed over
seven hundred people. How Daddy found these places was
always a mystery to us, but for the past two years, which
was a record, we had been living here in a small house we
rented. Since we didn't have all that much furniture anyway, it was quite adequate for our needs and the street was
quiet, the neighbors pleasant and friendly.

So here we were, hoping to stay, hoping to build a
life. Mommy was permitting herself to make close
friends, to join organizations, to make commitments. I
was doing well in school, and since I was at the beginning of my senior year, we were expecting I would graduate at this high school. I hadn't yet decided what I
wanted to do with my life. I had been in school plays and
I was told I had an impressive stage presence and carried
myself like a seasoned fashion model, but I knew I didn't
have a strong enough voice and I was never very comfortable memorizing lines and pretending to be someone
else.

Mommy didn't pressure me to be anything special. Her
advice was more along the lines of what to do with myself

socially. Lately, she was more strident sounding than ever with her warnings: "Don't give your heart to anyone until the last moment, and then think it over three times."

Her dark pronouncements came from her own regret in having married so young and ending what she called her chance for really living before she had even started. She and Daddy had been high-school sweethearts and consequently married soon after graduation, despite the admonishments of her parents, who refused to pay for a wedding. Daddy and she eloped and set up house as soon as he acquired the first of what was to be a long string of jobs.

Because of our lifestyle, I knew that Mommy now considered herself well beyond her prime. I could see it in her eyes whenever she and I went anywhere. She would take furtive glances at men to see if they were looking her way, following her movements with their eyes, showing any interest. If a younger woman pulled their attention from her, the disappointment would settle in her face like a rock in mud and she would want to get our shopping over quickly and go home to brood.

Over the years, she had taken odd jobs, working in department stores, especially in the cosmetic departments because she was a very attractive woman. When Daddy lost another position, Mommy would have to give up hers, no matter how well she was doing or how pleased her boss was with her work. After this happened a number of times, Mommy simply gave up trying to work.

"What's the point?" she asked Daddy. "I won't be able to hold down the job or get promoted."

"I'd rather have you at home anyway—my homemaker, Rose's full-time mother," Daddy declared avoiding any argument. He acted as if the added income was superfluous, when it sometimes was all we had.

Now, because we had lived in Lewisville so long, Mommy was considering returning to work. I was old enough to take care of my own needs, to help out in the house, and she had lots of free time to fill. Daddy didn't oppose her when she brought all this up now. In fact, they rarely had marital spats. Daddy was too easy for that. He would never disagree vehemently. Nothing seemed to matter that much to him, nothing deserved his raising his voice, putting on an angry face, sulking, or being in the slightest way unhappy. His reaction to it all was always a shrug and a simple "Whatever."

It had become our family motto. Whatever I wanted; whatever Mommy wanted. Whatever the world wanted of us, it was fine with Daddy. He loved that old adage, "If a branch doesn't bend, it breaks."

Whatever happened, happened. Forget it. Look to the future. It was a philosophy of life that turned every rainy day into a sunny one. You put your Band-Aids on your scrapes and bruises, choked back tears, and forgot about them.

"There should be only happy tears anyway," Daddy told me once. "What does crying get you? If you're miserable, you're defeating yourself. Laugh at life and you'll always be on top of things, Rose."

I looked at him with wonder, my daddy, the magician who seemed incapable of not finding rainbows. The ease with which he captured people impressed me, but what impressed me more was the ease with which he tossed it all away or gave it up once he had succeeded. Was that ability to let go with no regret a power or a madness? I wondered. Was nothing worth holding on to at any cost? Was nothing worth tears?

It wasn't long before I had an answer.

According to Mommy, it was Daddy who insisted on naming me Rose. It wasn't only because he insisted I had the sweetest face of any baby born that day. He argued that a rose always brought happiness, good times, bright wonderful things.

"What happens whenever you place a rose next to something?" he asked her in the hospital. "Huh? I'll tell you, Monica. It makes it seem more wonderful, more delicious, more enticing, and more desirable. That's what will happen every time she comes into a room or into anyone's life. That's our Rose."

Mommy said she gave in because she had never seen him so excited and determined about anything as much as he was about my name. She said my grandparents thought it was just dreadful to have a name like that on a birth certificate.

"She's a little girl, not a flower," Grandfather Wallace, Daddy's father, had declared. He favored old names, names garnered from ancestors, but Daddy had long since lost the ties with family that most people enjoy. His father never approved of the things he did with his life. Both of his parents closed all the blinds on every window that looked out on him. They shut down like clams, but Daddy didn't mourn the loss.

"People who drag you down, who are negative people, are dangerous," Daddy told me when I asked him about my grandparents and why we had so little to do with them. "Who needs that? Before long, they make you sad sacks, too. No sad sacks for us!" he cried, and swung me around.

When I was a little girl, he was always hugging me or twirling my strawberry-blond hair in his fingers, telling me that I was a jewel.

"Your eyes are two diamonds. Your hair is spun gold. Your lips are rubies and your skin comes from pearls. My rose petal," he cried, and kissed the tip of my nose. Laughter swirled in his eyes and dazzled me. Everything my daddy did was fascinating to me during those early years.

Not so my mother. Worry darkened her eyes. She took her deep breaths and waited, worked when she could, and made the best of every home we had, but I couldn't help feeling this same anxiety as I grew older and wiser and saw the shine begin to dull on Daddy's face and ways. Despite his attitudes and behavior, he was growing older. Gray hairs sounded small warnings and began to sprout like weeds in that flaxen cornfield. Lines deepened under his eyes. The world he had kept at bay was seeping under every door. He was beginning to show wear and tear. He had to search harder and harder to find ways to deny it or avoid it.

Daddy kept his little escapes private. He did a little more drinking than Mommy liked, but he didn't do it in saloons and dingy bars with degenerate friends. He kept his whiskey in a paper bag and drank surreptitiously. Even his drinking was solitary. All of his means of relaxation were. He loved to go duck hunting, but he never went with a group. He was a true loner when it came to all this. It was as if he didn't want to share those moments of doubt or admit that he needed his retreats from reality.

One weekend morning he rose early, as usual, and left the house before Mommy and I rose. He didn't leave a note or any indication where he had gone, but it was fall, and duck season, so we knew he was off to some solitary place he had discovered, some little outlet from which he could launch his rowboat and sit waiting for the ducks. He never shot more than we could eat, and Mommy was very good at preparing duck. She said it made him feel like some great hunter providing for his family. He was always saying that if we had to return to the days of the pioneers, he was equipped to do so.

The night before that, he had come into my room while I was doing my homework. He stood there awhile watching me quietly before I realized he had entered. He smiled at my surprise.

"Daddy? What?" I asked him.

He shook his head and sat beside me on the floor.

"Nothing in particular," Daddy replied. "But it's Friday night. How come you're not going anywhere with your friends—a movie, a dance? You're probably the most beautiful girl in the school."

"I'm going out with Paula Conrad tomorrow night, Daddy, remember?"

"Oh. Right."

He smiled.

"Just you and Paula?"

"We'll probably go to a movie and meet some other kids."

He nodded.

"And I assume other kids includes boys."

"Yes, Daddy."

"So how are you really doing these days, Rose? Are you happy here?"

A small patter of alarm began in my heart. Daddy often began a conversation this way when he was going to explain why we were about to move.

"Everything is good, Daddy. I like my teachers and I'm doing well in my classes. You saw my first report card this year: all A's. I've never gotten all A's before, Daddy," I pointed out.

He nodded, pressing his lips tightly.

"And I was in the school plays last year so I was thinking of going out for the big musical in the spring. The drama teacher keeps reminding me. I don't know why. I can't sing that well."

"You're the jewel, Rose. He wants his show to sparkle," Daddy said, smiling. "Don't be too humble," he warned. "Act like sheep and they'll act like wolves."

I knew he was right, but I was afraid to wish anything big for myself. I guess I've always been modest and shy. Maybe that was because I was afraid of committing myself to anything that required a long-term effort. We had been so nomadic, moving like gypsies from town to town, city to city, so often that I was terrified of becoming too close to anyone or too involved in any activity. Goodbyes were like tiny pins jabbed into my heart. How many times had I sat in the rear of the car looking through the back window at the home I had just known as it disappeared around a bend and was gone forever?

"I'm expecting you to become someone very special, Rose," Daddy told me as he sat there in my room. "I have high hopes. I know," he continued, "that I haven't exactly made things easy for you and your mother. But," he said, smiling, "you're like some powerful, magnificent flower plowing itself up between the rocks, finding the sunshine and blooming with blossoms richer than those of flowers in perfectly prepared gardens. Just believe in yourself," he advised.

Daddy hardly ever spoke so seriously to me. It kept my heart thumping.

"I'll try, Daddy," I said.

"Sure you will. Sure," he said. He played with the loose ends of my bedroom floor rug for a moment, holding his soft, gentle smile. "I guess I never had much faith in myself. I guess I move on so much because I'm afraid of making too much of an investment in anything. It would make failure look like failure," he said, looking up, "instead of just a temporary setback I could ignore.

"Don't be like me, Rose. Dig your heels into something and stick with it, okay?"

"Okay, Daddy," I said.

He stood up, leaned over and kissed me on the forehead, twirling my hair in his forefinger and reciting: "Your eyes are two diamonds. Your hair is spun gold. Your lips are rubies and your skin comes from pearls. My Rose petal."

He laughed, kissed me again and walked out.

I never heard his voice again.

POCKET BOOKS
PROUDLY PRESENTS

THE EXTRAORDINARY NOVEL
THAT HAS CAPTURED MILLIONS
IN ITS SPELL!

# *FLOWERS IN THE ATTIC*

# V.C. ANDREWS®

**Now available
in Mass Market from
Pocket Books**

**Turn the page for a preview of
*FLOWERS IN THE ATTIC....***

The train lumbered through a dark and starry night, heading toward a distant mountain estate in Virginia. We passed many a sleepy town and village, and scattered farmhouses where golden rectangles of light were the only evidence to show they were there at all. My brother and I didn't want to fall asleep and miss out on anything, and oh, did we have a lot to talk about! Mostly we speculated on that grand, rich house where we would live in splendor, and eat from golden plates, and be served by a butler wearing livery. And I supposed I'd have my own maid to lay out my clothes, draw my bath, brush my hair, and jump when I commanded.

While my brother and I speculated on how we would spend our money, the portly, balding conductor entered our small compartment and gazed admiringly at our mother before he softly spoke: "Mrs. Patterson, in fifteen minutes we'll reach your depot."

Now why was he calling her "Mrs. Patterson"? I wondered. I shot a questioning look at Christopher, who also seemed perplexed by this.

Jolted awake, appearing startled and disoriented, Momma's eyes flew wide open. Her gaze jumped from the conductor, who hovered so close above her, over to Christopher and me, and then she looked down in despair at the sleeping twins. "Yes, thank you," she said to the conductor, who was still watching her with great approval and admiration. "Don't fear, we'll be ready to leave."

"Ma'am," he said, most concerned when he glanced at his pocket watch, "it's three o'clock in the morning. Will someone be there to meet you?"

"It's all right," assured our mother.

"Ma'am, it's very dark out there."

"I could find my way home asleep."

The grandfatherly conductor wasn't satisfied with this. "Lady," he said, "we are letting you and your children off in the middle of nowhere. There's not a house in sight."

To forbid any further questioning, Momma answered in her most arrogant manner, "Someone *is* meeting us." Funny how she could put on that kind of haughty manner like a hat.

It was totally dark when we stepped from the train, and as the conductor had warned, there was not a house in sight. Alone in the night, far from any sign of civilization, we stood and waved good-bye to the conductor on the train steps, holding on by one hand, waving with the other. His expression revealed that he wasn't too happy about leaving "Mrs. Patterson" and her brood of four sleepy children waiting for someone coming in a car. I looked around and saw nothing but a rusty, tin roof supported by four wooden posts, and a rickety green bench.

We were surrounded by fields and meadows. From the deep woods in back of the "depot," something made a weird noise. I jumped and spun about to see what it was, making Christopher laugh. "That was only an owl! Did you think it was a ghost?"

"Now there is to be none of that!" said Momma sharply. "We have to hurry. It's a long, long walk to my home, and we have to reach there before dawn, when the servants get up."

How strange. "Why?" I asked. "And why did that conductor call you Mrs. Patterson?"

"Cathy, I don't have time to explain to you now. We've got to walk fast." She bent to pick up the two heaviest suitcases. Christopher and I were forced to carry the twins, who were too sleepy to walk.

"Momma!" I cried out, when we had moved on a few steps, "the conductor forgot to give us *your* two suitcases!"

"It's all right, Cathy," she said breathlessly, as if the two suitcases she was carrying were enough to tax her strength. "I asked the conductor to take my two bags on to Charlottesville and put them in a locker for me to pick up tomorrow morning."

"Why would you do that?" asked Christopher.

"Well, for one thing, I certainly couldn't handle *four* suitcases, could I? And, for another thing, I want the chance to talk to my father first before he learns about you. And it just wouldn't seem right if I arrived home in the middle of the night after being gone for fifteen years, now would it?"

It sounded reasonable, I guess, for we did have all we could handle. We set off, tagging along behind our mother, over uneven ground, following faint paths between rocks and trees and shrubbery that clawed at our clothes. We trekked a long, long way. Christopher and I became tired, irritable, as the twins grew heavier, and our arms began to ache. We complained, we nagged, we dragged our feet, wanting to sit down and rest. We wanted to be back in our own beds, with our own things—better than here—better than that big old house with servants and grandparents we didn't even know.

"Wake up the twins!" snapped Momma, grown impatient with our complaining. "Stand them on their feet, and force them to walk." Then she mumbled something faint into the collar of her jacket that just barely reached my ears: "Lord knows, they'd better walk outside while they can."

A ripple of apprehension shot down my spine. I glanced at my older brother to see if he'd heard, just as he turned his head to look at me. He smiled. I smiled in return.

Tomorrow, when Momma arrived at a proper time, in a taxi, she would go to the sick grandfather and she'd smile, and she'd speak, and he'd be charmed, won over. Just one look at her lovely face, and just one word from her soft beautiful voice, and he'd hold out his arms, and forgive her for whatever she'd done to make her "fall from grace."

From what she'd already told us, her father was a cantankerous *old* man, for sixty-six did seem like incredibly old age to me. And a man on the verge of death couldn't afford to hold grudges against his sole remaining child, a daughter he'd once loved very much. Then she'd bring us down from the bedroom, and we'd be looking our best, and acting our sweetest selves, and he'd soon see we weren't ugly, or really bad, and nobody, absolutely nobody with a heart could resist loving the twins. And just wait until Grandfather learned how smart Christopher was!

The air was cool and sharply pungent. Though Momma called this hill country, those shadowy, high forms in the distance looked like mountains to me. I stared up at the sky. Why did it seem to be looking down at me with pity, making me feel ant-sized, overwhelmed, completely insignificant? It was too big, that sky, too beautiful, and it filled me with a strange sense of foreboding.

We came at last upon a cluster of large and very fine homes, nestled on a steep hillside. Stealthily, we approached the largest and, by far, the grandest of all the sleeping mountain homes.

We circled that enormous house, almost on tiptoes. At the back door, an old lady let us in. She must have been waiting, and seen us coming, for she opened that door so readily we didn't even have to knock. Just like thieves in the night, we stole silently inside. Not a word did she speak to welcome us. Could this be one of the servants? I wondered.

Immediately we were inside the dark house, and she hustled us up a steep and narrow back staircase, not allowing us one second to pause and take a look around the grand rooms we only glimpsed in our swift passage. She led us down many halls, past many closed doors, and finally we came to an end room, where she swung open a door and gestured us inside. It was a relief to have our long night journey over, and be in a large bedroom where a single lamp was lit. The old woman turned to look us over as she closed the heavy door to the hall and leaned against it.

She spoke, and I was jolted. "Just as you said, Corrine. Your children are beautiful."

There she was, paying us a compliment that should warm our hearts—but it chilled mine. Her voice was cold and uncaring, as if we were without ears to hear, and without minds to comprehend her displeasure, despite her flattery.

"But are you sure they are intelligent? Do they have some invisible afflictions not apparent to the eyes?"

"None!" cried our mother, taking offense, as did I. "My children are perfect, as you can plainly see, physically and mentally!" She glared at that old woman in gray before she squatted down on her heels and began to undress Carrie, who was nodding on her feet. I knelt before Cory and unbuttoned his small blue jacket, as Christopher lifted one of the suitcases up on one of the big beds. He opened it and took out two pairs of small yellow pajamas with feet.

Furtively, as I helped Cory off with his clothes and into his yellow pajamas, I studied that tall, big woman, who was, I presumed, our grandmother.

Her nose was an eagle's beak, her shoulders were wide, and her mouth was like a thin, crooked knife slash. Her dress, of gray taffeta, had a diamond brooch at the throat of a high, severe neckline. Nothing about her appeared soft or yielding; even her bosom looked like twin hills of concrete. There would be no funning with her, as we had played with our mother and father.

I didn't like her. I wanted to go home. My lips quivered.

How could such a woman as this make someone as lovely and sweet as our mother? From whom had our mother inherited her beauty, her gaiety? I shivered, and tried to forbid those tears that welled in my eyes. Momma had prepared us in advance for an unloving, uncaring, unrelenting grandfather—but the grandmother who had arranged for our coming—she came as a harsh, astonishing surprise. I blinked back my tears. But to reassure me, there was our mother smiling warmly as she lifted a pajamaed Cory into one of the big beds, and then she put Carrie in beside him. Oh, how they did look sweet, lying there, like big, rosy-cheeked dolls. Momma leaned over the twins and pressed kisses on their flushed cheeks, and her hand tenderly brushed back the curls on their foreheads. "Good night, my darlings," she whispered in the loving voice we knew so well.

The twins didn't hear. Already they were deeply asleep.

However, standing firmly as a rooted tree, the grandmother was obviously displeased as she gazed upon the twins in one bed, then over to where Christopher and I were huddled close together. We were tired, and half-supporting each other. Strong disapproval glinted in her gray-stone eyes; Momma seemed to understand, although I did not. Momma's face flushed as the grandmother said, "Your two older children cannot sleep in one bed!"

"They're only children," Momma flared back with unusual fire. "You have a nasty, suspicious mind! Christopher and Cathy are innocent!"

"Innocent?" she snapped back, her mean look so sharp it could cut and draw blood. "That is exactly what your father and I always presumed about you and your half-uncle!"

"If you think like that, then give them separate rooms and separate beds."

"That is impossible," the grandmother said. "This is the only bedroom with its own adjoining bath, and where my husband won't hear them walking overhead, or flushing the toilet. If they are separated, and scattered about all over upstairs, he will hear their voices, or their noise, or the servants will. This is the only safe room."

Safe room? We were going to sleep, all of us, in only one room? In a grand, rich house with twenty, thirty, forty rooms, we were going to stay in one room? Even so, now that I gave it more thought, I didn't want to be in a room alone in this mammoth house.

"Put the two girls in one bed, and the two boys in the other," the grandmother ordered.

Momma lifted Cory and put him in the remaining double bed, thus, casually establishing the way it was to be from then on.

The old woman turned her hard gaze on me, then on Christopher. "Now hear this," she began like a drill sergeant, "it will be up to you two older children to keep the younger ones quiet. Keep this always in your minds: if your grandfather learns you are up here, then he will throw all of you out without one red penny—*after* he has severely punished you for being alive! You will not yell, or cry, or run about to pound on the ceilings below. When your mother and I leave this room tonight, I will close and lock the door behind me. Until the day your grandfather dies, you are here, but you don't really exist."

Oh, God! This couldn't be true! She was lying, wasn't she? Saying mean things just to scare us. I tried to look at Momma, but she had turned her back and her head was lowered, but her shoulders sagged and quivered as if she were crying.

Panic filled me....